MICHAEL CRICHTON

Jurassic Park

Retold by F.H. Cornish

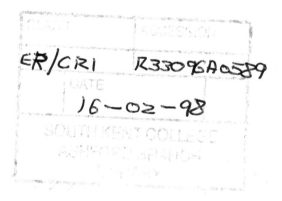

HEINEMANN

INTERMEDIATE LEVEL

Series Editor: John Milne

The Heinemann Guided Readers provide a choice of enjoyable reading material for learners of English. The Series is published at five levels – Starter, Beginner, Elementary, Intermediate and Upper. At **Intermediate Level**, the control of content and language has the following main features:

Information Control
Information which is vital to the understanding of the story is presented in an easily assimilated manner and is repeated when necessary. Difficult allusion and metaphor are avoided and cultural backgrounds are made explicit.

Structure Control
Most of the structures used in the Readers will be familiar to students who have completed an elementary course of English. Other grammatical features may occur, but their use is made clear through context and reinforcement. This ensures that the reading, as well as being enjoyable, provides a continual learning situation for the students. Sentences are limited in most cases to a maximum of three clauses and within sentences there is a balanced use of adverbial and adjectival phrases. Great care is taken with pronoun reference.

Vocabulary Control
There is a basic vocabulary of approximately 1600 words. Help is given to the students in the form of illustrations, which are closely related to the text.

Glossary
Some difficult words and phrases in this book are important for understanding the story. Some of these words are explained in the story, some are shown in the pictures, and others are marked with a number like this ... [3]. Words with a number are explained in the Glossary on page 118.

Contents

A Note About This Story

Michael Crichton wrote this story in 1991. It was made into a very exciting film in 1993 by Steven Spielberg. It became the most successful and famous movie ever made. The film has been seen by millions of people in many countries all over the world.

For many hundreds of years, people have been interested in the bones of huge animals that they have found in the ground. In some countries, people thought that these were the bodies of dragons – powerful, magical creatures.

Today, we know that these are the bones of dinosaurs. Dinosaurs lived between about 245 and 64 million years ago. The scientists who dig up dinosaurs' bones and study them are called paleontologists[1]. They look for the bones of dinosaurs in many countries in the world. The bones have been in the ground for millions of years and they have become fossilized – hard like stone. A great number of fossils[2] from dinosaurs have been found in Europe, in the south of the USA, and in the deserts and mountains of Asia. There are dinosaur skeletons in many museums all over the world and many thousands of people go to look at them.

Paleobotanists[3] often work with paleontologists. They also dig in the ground and look for fossilized plants and trees that were alive millions of years ago. They study these fossils to find out more about prehistoric life.

Dinosaurs were the largest creatures that ever lived on the Earth. Some of them were bigger than houses. But there were small dinosaurs too. Many dinosaurs have names which are long and rather difficult to say! Look at the list on pages

116-117 of this book to help you.

Paleontologists say that dinosaurs came from different families. They think that some dinosaurs had bodies like birds and others had bodies like reptiles such as snakes and lizards. At one time, scientists thought that all dinosaurs were like reptiles. They believed that these huge animals were very slow and stupid. They also thought that dinosaurs needed the warmth of the sun to help them to move. But now, many paleontologists think that dinosaurs were more like birds. They believed that they moved quickly, they lived in groups and looked for food together. The babies were born from eggs and the adults looked after them carefully.

Dinosaurs were either plant-eaters or meat-eaters. Plant-eating dinosaurs were enormous and moved together in large groups. They ate the leaves and branches of trees in the forests and the plants in the lakes. Meat-eating dinosaurs were extremely strong and fierce. They probably did not live in large groups. They could run fast and they hunted the plant-eating dinosaurs. They used their sharp teeth and claws to catch and eat them.

People all over the world are fascinated by dinosaurs. And scientists try to answer their questions. What did they look like? When did they live? What did they eat? How did they behave[4]? Why did they all die?

This story is not true. There are no living dinosaurs. But who knows what might happen in the future?

The People in This Story

◄ **Dr Alan Grant**
a paleontologist

Dr Ellie Sattler ►
a paleobotanist

◄ **Bob Morris**
a lawyer[5],
the Environmental
Protection Agency[6]

Donald Gennaro ►
a lawyer,
InGen Incorporated

◄ **Dennis Nedry**
a computer expert[7]

Professor Ian Malcolm
a mathematician[8]

John Hammond ▶
a millionaire,
the owner of
Jurassic Park

Ed Regis ◀
the publicity manager[9]

John Arnold ▶
the chief engineer[10]

◀ **Robert Muldoon**
the park warden[11]

Henry Wu ▶
the chief geneticist[12]

◀ **Dr Harding**
the vet[13] (veterinary surgeon)

Tim Murphy ▶
◀ **Lex Murphy**
John Hammond's grandchildren

1

The Dinosaur Hunters

Wednesday: Snakewater, Montana, USA

The temperature was over 40°C. The hot sun shone on the hills and rocks. Alan Grant was kneeling on the ground brushing dust away from a tiny bone. It was a bone from a dinosaur which had lived 75 million years ago.

'Alan! Alan!'

He looked up and saw Ellie waving[14] to him.

'Alan!' she shouted again. 'The lawyer from the EPA has arrived.'

'Why does a lawyer from the Environmental Protection Agency want to talk to me?' thought Grant. He stood up and went down the hill to meet his visitor.

A man was standing by a car in the bright sunshine.

'I'm Bob Morris,' said the visitor, shaking hands with Grant. 'You must be Dr Alan Grant.'

'That's right. I am a paleontologist,' replied Grant. 'And this is Ellie Sattler. She's a paleobotanist.'

'I study plants from the time of the dinosaurs,' explained Ellie. 'And I also help Alan study the bones that we find.' She shook hands with Bob Morris. 'Come into our office.'

They went into a trailer and the two men sat down. Ellie went to the other end of the trailer and started examining some small bones.

'I want to ask you about John Hammond,' said Morris. 'The EPA is interested in finding out more about him. You get some money from him, don't you?'

'Alan!' Ellie shouted. 'The lawyer from the EPA has arrived.'

'Yes, he gives us about $30000 a year for our work on dinosaurs,' replied Grant.

'What do you know about Hammond?'

'Well, he's very rich and he is very interested in dinosaurs. Mr Hammond gives money to people doing research on dinosaurs.'

'Do you know why he is also interested in amber[15]?' asked Morris.

'Amber?'

'Yes. It's a hard yellow substance – dried sap from trees —'

'I know what amber is,' Grant said. 'But amber has no connection with[16] dinosaurs. Why are you asking?'

'Because in the last five years,' Morris went on, 'Hammond has spent $17 million buying amber. And there's another strange thing. What do you know about Hammond's island near Costa Rica? Ten years ago Hammond bought it from the Costa Rican government.'

'I don't know anything about it,' said Grant.

'The island is 160 km from Costa Rica,' explained Morris. 'It's called Isla Nublar, or Cloud Island, because it's always covered in thick fog. You were paid to do some work in connection with this island.'

'Was I?' asked Grant. He was surprised.

Morris gave Grant a piece of paper. It was a copy of a cheque paid to Grant by InGen Incorporated. On it was written: ALAN GRANT/CONSULTANT/ISLA NUBLAR.

'InGen is one of Hammond's companies,' Morris said.

'Oh, I remember,' said Grant. 'InGen did pay me to be a consultant. But the work wasn't anything to do with an island. A man called Donald Gennaro phoned me —'

'Gennaro works for InGen's lawyers,' said Morris. 'What

did he want?'

'He wanted me to tell him about how dinosaurs lived. I have done a lot of research on dinosaur eggs and young dinosaurs. Gennaro said he would pay me $50 000. He said he was planning a museum for children. He was paying other consultants too – a mathematician called Ian Malcolm and some computer experts.'

'What information did you give him?'

'I told him about dinosaurs' nests, eggs and food. And I told him what I guessed about the behaviour of adult dinosaurs with young ones. But he phoned me all the time – day and night. Would dinosaurs eat this? Would they eat that? I couldn't understand why he was so worried. The work was taking too much time so I stopped doing it. InGen paid me $12 000 for the work I did.'

'And do you know anything more about John Hammond?'

'No – why don't you speak to Hammond yourself?'

'The EPA can't speak to him at the moment. The EPA thinks that Hammond is doing something wrong, but we aren't sure yet.

'InGen has sent two very powerful Cray XMP supercomputers[17] to Isla Nublar,' Morris went on. 'And they have sent Hood gene sequencers[18] there too. Each machine costs half a million dollars and they have sent *twenty-four* to Isla Nublar. Why?'

'I don't know,' said Grant.

'Hood gene sequencers are machines that find genetic sequences from samples of DNA[19],' continued Morris. 'There are companies that want to do genetic engineering which is dangerous. So these companies go to countries where there are no laws about genetic engineering. We are very worried.

We want to know what InGen and Hammond are doing on Isla Nublar.'

They went out of the office into the hot sunshine.

'Well, thank you for your help, Dr Grant,' said Morris and he drove off.

As Grant started to walk back to the office, Ellie came to the door.

'I've just had a phone call,' she said. 'It was from a doctor at Columbia University. She's sending you a fax[20]. She'd like you to look at it and speak to her.'

——

'My God!' said Grant. He was staring at a fax of an X-ray[21]. Ellie was staring at it too.

'There hasn't been a lizard like this on Earth for more than 200 million years. Lizards like this lived in the Triassic Period[22],' said Grant. 'This looks like a *compsognathus*[23], a young one, about 30 cm tall.'

Ellie read out the note which came with the X-ray. 'It says, "Lizard found on Cabo Blanco Beach in Costa Rica. Part of its body has been eaten by a monkey. A lizard like this attacked a 10-year-old girl on the same beach. There have also been reports about lizards attacking babies."'

'Is this a fake, Alan?' Ellie asked. 'Is someone making a joke? Or is this a real[24] animal?'

'I don't know,' said Grant. 'Most dinosaurs were living in the Jurassic Period[25] – about 190 million years ago. But compsognathids were alive a long time before that. They come from the Triassic Period – about 220 million years ago. And some animals from the Triassic Period still live in the world today. Crocodiles and sharks[26] haven't changed for more than 220 million years.'

The phone rang. 'That will be the doctor who sent the fax,' said Grant. 'Perhaps she can tell us more about this lizard.'

He answered the phone. But it wasn't the doctor who was phoning. 'Mr Hammond!' said Grant in surprise. He pressed a button on the phone so Ellie could also hear the conversation. She heard an old man's voice speaking angrily.

'— A man called Morris has been asking questions. He's been talking to Ian Malcolm. Has he been to see you?'

'Yes,' said Grant, 'he has.'

'I think Morris wants to go to Costa Rica, to our island down there,' said Hammond. 'I own an island called Isla Nublar. I bought it about ten years ago. Isla Nublar is going to be a resort and animal park[27]. I've sent you some information about it. Have you received it?'

'No, but — '

'Oh, well, you'll get the parcel tomorrow,' Hammond went on, speaking very quickly. 'It's a big resort and we're going to open it soon. You will be very interested, Dr Grant. I want you to come to the island this weekend to see my park. I'll pay you to be a consultant. I'd like to know what you think about my work. I'd like your opinion.'

'I'm sorry, but I can't come,' replied Grant. 'I'm very busy here and I've just received information about a living compsognathus.'

'A living compsognathus! Where did it come from?'

'From a beach called Cabo Blanco on Costa Rica —'

'Dr Grant, have you told anyone about this?'

'No.'

'Good. Good. Dr Grant, I want you to come to my island. I'd like Dr Sattler to come to the island too. I'll pay you both to be consultants for three days. I'll pay you $60 000 each. Will you come?'

'OK, Mr Hammond,' said Grant. 'That much money will pay for our research for the next two years.'

'Good. Good,' said Hammond. 'Go to Choteau airport at 5 p.m. tomorrow evening. I'll be waiting for you.'

2

The Consultants

Thursday: a lawyer's office, San Francisco, USA

'We've got to look at the island now,' said Donald Gennaro to his boss. 'There are too many problems. The Environmental Protection Agency is asking questions about Hammond. Workmen have died on the island. The computer systems[28] don't work properly and the resort isn't going to open on time. And now someone has found a lizard which is biting children in Costa Rica. A lot of people have invested[29] money in Hammond's resort. We can't let things go wrong now.'

'I agree,' said his boss. 'You must go to Isla Nublar now. I want the problems on the island put right in a week. Who is going with you?'

'A paleontologist, a paleobotanist and a mathematician. I'm going there this weekend with them. Hammond invited them himself. He says that there are no problems. He's told them that he wants them to see his new resort. A computer expert is going too. He's going to sort out the bugs in the computer system[30].'

Thursday: Snakewater, Montana

Ellie Sattler and Alan Grant were looking at the parcel of information which Hammond had sent about Isla Nublar. There were plans of buildings and a map. The map showed that the island was long and narrow. There were roads and tunnels and a lake. There was a Visitors' Centre in the north and the island was divided into five sections[31]. Between the sections there were roads. Between the roads and the sections there were concrete moats[32] and electric fences[33].

'It's like a zoo,' said Ellie. 'The roads are high up so you can see over the fences and the moats. But everything is enormous – there's a moat which is 9 m wide!'

'And all these buildings are made of concrete and have thick walls,' said Grant.

'We've got to go now, Alan,' said Ellie, looking at her watch. 'We've got to get to the airport at Choteau by five o'clock.'

Thursday: going to Isla Nublar

Gennaro was sitting with John Hammond on Hammond's plane. Hammond was a small man, about 75 years old. The plane had just taken off from San Francisco airport.

'Is the resort ready for visitors?' Gennaro asked.

'No, not quite. But the Safari Lodge is ready.'

'And the animals? I remember that you wanted to have twelve.'

'Oh, we've got far more than that. We've got 238. There are 15 different species,' replied Hammond.

'Two hundred and thirty-eight!'

The old man laughed. 'So, you see there is no problem with Isla Nublar. There are places to stay, lots of animals and the most modern computers to run everything. We will make a lot of money.'

John Hammond's plane landed at Choteau, in Montana, late in the afternoon. Ellie and Grant got on.

'Dr Grant and Dr Sattler,' said Hammond, 'I'm pleased you've come. Let me introduce you to Donald Gennaro.'

Donald Gennaro shook hands with Alan Grant and Ellie Sattler. He was about 30 years old and he was wearing an expensive grey suit and glasses with metal frames. Grant didn't like him.

Thursday: San Francisco Airport

A man was waiting in a café for the lawyer from the Biosyn Corporation. The man worked for the genetic engineering company, InGen. He was going to steal something from InGen for the Biosyn Corporation. Biosyn was going to pay him $1 500 000. Biosyn was also a genetic engineering company. Biosyn knew all about Hammond's resort on Isla Nublar.

The lawyer from Biosyn arrived. He was carrying a briefcase. Inside it was $750 000 – half of the money.

'Remember, I want samples of all 15 species,' he said.

'I remember,' said the man from InGen. 'You want the embryos of all 15 species[34]. How am I going to carry them?'

The lawyer gave him a large canister of shaving foam[35]. 'The top part of the canister has foam in it. The bottom part is empty,' he said. 'If the authorities look in your case at the airport there won't be a problem. You can put all the embryos in the bottom of the canister. No one will know what you are hiding there.

'You can keep the embryos in this canister for 36 hours,' the lawyer went on. 'There will be a boat at the east dock[36] of the island on Friday night. Don't go to the big dock at the north end of the island. You must go to the east dock. The boat will take the canister to San José in Costa Rica. Do you understand?'

'Yes. Yes,' said the man from InGen. 'I'll be back in San José on Sunday. You can give me the other $750 000 – the rest of my money, then.'

Thursday: going to Isla Nublar

Hammond's plane landed at Dallas airport four hours after it left Choteau. A tall, thin man got on. He was about 35 years old. Everything he was wearing was black. He was a university professor but he looked like a rock star.

'Hello, Professor Malcolm,' said Hammond.

Malcolm smiled and introduced himself to everyone. 'I'm Ian Malcolm. How do you do? I do maths.'

Grant had heard about Professor Malcolm. He was a famous mathematician. He was interested in how the world worked. He studied something called the chaos theory.

'It's a good thing you invited me to come,' said Malcolm to Hammond. 'I've heard that you have a serious problem on your island.'

'There's no problem,' said Hammond angrily.

'I told you that your resort wouldn't work,' said Malcolm. 'You'll have to close it. I've brought copies of the report I wrote for InGen five years ago. You can read the report again.'

Hammond stood up. Angrily, he went to sit in another part of the plane.

'I've heard that you have a serious problem on your island,'
said Malcolm.

It was a long journey and Grant tried to read Malcolm's report for InGen. It was very difficult to understand. At last, he spoke to Malcolm.

'Your report says that Hammond's resort on the island will never work – because of chaos theory. I don't understand. Can you explain chaos theory to me, please?'

'Yes. All right ... Here is an example. The weather is a complex system[37]. Scientists used to say that they could not predict[38] the weather because they didn't understand complex systems. Now scientists understand a lot more about complex systems but they still can't predict the weather. OK?'

'OK. I understand that,' said Grant.

'Scientists have now learnt *why* they can't predict the weather,' continued Malcolm. 'They've learnt that very small changes are always happening in complex systems. These changes can't be predicted. These changes make something else change and then something else changes and so on.

'If scientists do an experiment on a complex system and then repeat the same experiment they get very different results. This is because of all these tiny unpredictable changes. Chaos theory is about all the unpredictable changes we find in complex systems.'

'OK,' said Grant again.

'Hammond's island is unpredictable,' said Malcolm. 'He has animals on his island. It's like a zoo. You may think this is a simple system. But you cannot predict what will happen with animals and living things. Hammond's company, InGen, has tried to make the island safe in lots of ways. But I know things will happen that no one can predict. Things will start to go wrong and they will continue to go wrong.'

3

Isla Nublar

Early on Friday morning, Hammond's plane landed at San José, the biggest city in Costa Rica. Then Grant, Ellie, Malcolm, Gennaro and Hammond got into a small helicopter to fly to Isla Nublar. The island was 160 km away. Another man got on the helicopter with them. His name was Dennis Nedry and he was fat and unfriendly. He said that he was a computer expert. He said that he was going to the island to sort out some bugs in the computer system.

After 45 minutes, they saw the island. It had steep sides and there were thick forests. There were clouds of fog all round the island. The helicopter flew towards the northern end of the island.

'The island is about 12 km long and 5 km wide,' said Hammond. 'And the hills are about 600 m high at this end of the island. We're going to land now.'

Suddenly the helicopter went straight down through the fog. It landed on top of one of the hills. As the visitors got out of the helicopter, a man wearing a baseball cap ran up to them.

'Hi!' he said. 'I'm Ed Regis – the publicity manager. It's my job to look after visitors to the resort. Welcome to Isla Nublar.'

They all started to walk down the hill. Grant looked around him. He looked down the hill towards the south of the island then he stopped and stared. He could see a tall, curved[39] tree trunk in the distance. But it had no leaves and it was taller than all the other trees. Then the tree trunk moved and turned towards Grant.

Suddenly, the paleontologist realized that he wasn't looking at a tree trunk. He was looking at the curved neck of an animal 15 m high. He was looking at a dinosaur!

'My God!' said Ellie Sattler quietly. 'It's beautiful. It moves so gracefully.'

Gennaro had known for years what Hammond had been doing on Isla Nublar. But he had never believed it. He didn't say anything, but he had two thoughts: 'We're going to make billions[40] of dollars from this place' and, 'I hope the island is safe'.

Grant felt strange. He could not believe what he was seeing. How had Hammond made this animal?

The dinosaur made a loud trumpeting[41] sound and more heads moved up above the trees.

They are *apatosaurs*[42], thought Grant. They move more quickly than I thought they would. Then he laughed. He was starting to believe that these animals were real.

'Hammond, they are machines, aren't they?' asked Malcolm.

'No, Professor Malcolm,' replied Hammond, smiling. 'They are alive.'

There were more trumpeting sounds from the apatosaurs.

'They're welcoming you to the island,' said Ed Regis.

'Go with Mr Regis,' said Hammond. 'He'll show you to your rooms in the Safari Lodge. I'll see you later.'

As they went down the hill towards some buildings, they passed a sign which said: WELCOME TO JURASSIC PARK.

'Your work will change now,' said Malcolm to Grant. 'You can study living dinosaurs, not the bones of dead ones.'

He was looking at the curved neck of an animal 15 m high.
He was looking at a dinosaur!

'Yes,' said Grant. 'But how did InGen make these apatosaurs? Where did they get the dinosaur DNA? You need DNA to make a living thing. You can't get DNA from fossils. No one has ever found a whole body of a dinosaur. So how did they get dinosaur DNA?

'Genetic engineers are making new discoveries about DNA all the time,' Grant went on. 'Have they found a way to make dinosaur DNA? Without the correct DNA they cannot make real dinosaurs.'

'Well, everything looks right,' said Ellie. 'Not only the dinosaurs. The plants and trees are correct for the Jurassic Period.'

'It's amazing, isn't it?' said Ed Regis. 'Look! This is where you will be staying – the Safari Lodge.' And he pointed at a building at the bottom of the hill.

———

Later, at the Safari Lodge, Ellie and Grant remembered the plans which Hammond had sent them.

'These buildings don't look like the ones on the plans,' said Ellie. 'The windows are all small and there are bars over them. The doors are made of metal. And look at the sky-lights[43] on the roof. There are bars over the skylights too.'

'And there's a fence made from thick metal bars around the lodge,' said Grant. 'Those plans showed a hotel. This is like a prison and I want to know why. Hammond can tell me – the tour[44] starts in 20 minutes.'

———

Grant and Ellie met Malcolm, Regis, Gennaro, Nedry and Hammond again in the Visitors' Centre. It was a two-storeyed building[45] next to the Safari Lodge. They went into a room where there was an exhibition. There were chairs, pictures on the walls and a big sign saying: WHEN DINOSAURS RULED THE EARTH. There was also a model of a *tyrannosaurus rex*[46]. They sat down and Gennaro stood and spoke to them.

'Hammond and his scientists will tell you that everything works well here,' he said. 'But you are experts and I want your opinions. You know now that this is a park where dinosaurs live in special enclosures. These living dinosaurs have been made by genetic engineering. The park is going to be open for visitors in a year's time.

'I want the answers to some questions,' Gennaro went on. 'Is the island safe for visitors? Are the dinosaurs kept safely on the island? Are the security systems[47] and all the enclosures strong enough? Will the dinosaurs be unable to escape from the island?'

'The answer to each question is no,' said Malcolm. 'I explained that. My theory predicts that things will go wrong.'

'I am worried,' said Gennaro, 'because I have heard about strange lizards biting children in Costa Rica. Also, Dr Grant has seen a fax of an X-ray of one of these lizards. He thinks it looks like a small dinosaur.'

'It's possible that a few animals have escaped,' said Grant.

Hammond stood up and went out of the room noisily. Then suddenly, they heard the sound of a helicopter.

'I wonder who is coming?' said Gennaro.

They all went outside. Hammond joined them. When the helicopter landed, Ed Regis went to meet the people who got out. There were two children. One was a boy who was about 11 years old. He was wearing glasses and he looked very serious. The other child was a girl, about 8 years old. Her hair was blonde and she was wearing a baseball cap.

'Hi, Grandpa, we're here!' she shouted, and she waved to

Hammond.

'These are my grandchildren, Tim and Lex Murphy,' Hammond said to everyone. 'They've come to spend the weekend here.'

Gennaro was angry with Hammond. 'This is not a holiday,' he said. 'My company is worried about the safety of this island. I am here to find out if the island is safe. We might have to close your park down if I find out it isn't safe. Now you've brought these children here and they might be in danger.'

But Hammond wouldn't listen to Gennaro. He became angry again. He started to walk back to the Safari Lodge.

'I'll see you at dinner this evening,' he said. 'Ed will show you everything and take you on a tour of the island.'

Tim looked at all the adults. There was Ed, who had met them when they got off the helicopter. There was an unfriendly fat man and the man in a grey suit who had been angry with Grandpa. Then there was a thin man dressed in black clothes, a pretty woman with blonde hair, and another man. This man had sun-tanned skin and blue eyes. Suddenly, Tim recognized the man with the sun-tanned skin.

'You're Dr Alan Grant, the paleontologist,' Tim said. 'I've read your book – *The Lost World of the Dinosaurs*. I love dinosaurs.'

'Perhaps we will learn a lot more about dinosaurs now,' said Grant.

'Why?' asked Tim.

'Because of what's happening here on your grandfather's island,' replied Grant.

Tim did not understand. 'My Mum said the island was a holiday resort,' he said.

4

How to Make a Dinosaur

Regis, Nedry, Ellie and Malcolm went back into the Visitors' Centre and up some stairs. Grant, Tim and Lex followed them. They passed a large sign saying: NO ENTRY. AUTHORIZED[48] PEOPLE ONLY.

'The whole island is controlled from the first floor of this building,' said Ed Regis.

They stopped outside a room and looked in through some windows at the people working inside.

'This is the Control Room and that's John Arnold, the chief engineer,' Regis said. He pointed to a thin man in a white coat. 'And that big man is Robert Muldoon. He's the park warden who looks after all the animals. They're two of the most important men in Jurassic Park. The other important man is Dr Harding who is the vet. He's out in the park now. He's looking after a sick animal. We'll come back here soon. But first, I want to show you how we make the dinosaurs.'

Soon they reached a door with a sign on it saying: EXTRACTIONS[49]. Regis used a security card[50] to unlock the door and they all went into a small room. Inside, there were microscopes[51] and shelves full of yellow stones.

Regis introduced them to a short man who was about 30 years old. 'This is Henry Wu,' he said. 'He's our chief geneticist. He knows all about the genetic engineering we do here.'

'We want to know where you get dinosaur DNA from,' said Ellie.

Wu picked up one of the yellow stones. 'We get it from here,' he said. 'We get the DNA from amber. Many millions of years ago the sap from trees hardened – became fossilized. This hard substance is called amber.

'Sometimes the sticky sap from these trees caught insects before it became hard like this. Some of these insects had fed on animals – dinosaurs. So dinosaur blood is inside these insects. Come and look.'

Dr Wu took the visitors to a microscope. When they looked through the microscope they saw a small fly in a piece of amber. Dr Wu pushed a long needle[52] into the amber and the fly. Then he was able to extract some blood from the fly.

'We've been extracting blood from insects in amber for five years,' he said. 'We're trying to collect dinosaur blood. Now, come in here, and see what we do next.'

Wu led them into a much bigger room. There was a loud humming[53] sound coming from the machines in the room. There were big metal boxes around the walls of the room and in the middle there were two tall towers.

'The boxes are Hood gene sequencers and the towers in the middle are Cray XMP supercomputers,' said Wu. 'These machines are very powerful. It used to take many weeks to do the work that these computers can do in a few hours. They work on the DNA from the blood and they repair the DNA chains. The chains need repairing because we only find small pieces of dinosaur DNA in the blood from the flies. We cannot find the whole chain. Look at this screen and I'll show you what I mean.'

'These letters on the screen show a tiny piece of dinosaur DNA,' Wu said. 'We need to make a whole chain of dinosaur DNA.

```
1      GCGTTGCTGG  CGTTTTTCCA  TAGGCTCCGC  CCCCCTGACG  AGCATCACAA  AAATCGACGC
61     GGTGGCGAAA  CCCGACAGGA  CTATAAAGAT  ACCAGGCGTT  TCCCCCTGGA  AGCTCCCTCG
121    TGTTCCGACC  CTGCCGCTTA  CCGGATACCT  GTCCGCCTTT  CTCCCTTCGG  GAAGCGTGGC
181    TGCTCACGCT  GTAGGTATCT  CAGTTCGGTG  TAGGTCGTTC  GCTCCAAGCT  GGGCTGTGTG
241    CCGTTCAGCC  CGACCGCTGC  GCCTTATCCG  GTAACTATCG  TCTTGAGTCC  AACCCGGTAA
301    AGTAGGACAG  GTGCCGGCAG  CGCTCTGGGT  CATTTTCGGC  GAGGACCGCT  TTCGCTGGAG
361    ATCGGCCTGT  CGCTTGCGGT  ATTCGGAATC  TTGCACGCCC  TCGCTCAAGC  CTTCGTCACT
421    CCAAACGTTT  CGGCGAGAAG  CAGGCCATTA  TCGCCGGCAT  GGCGGCCGAC  GCGCTGGGCT
481    GGCGTTCGCG  ACGCGAGGCT  GGATGGCCTT  CCCCATTATG  ATTCTTCTCG  CTTCCGGCGG
541    CCCGCGTTGC  AGGCCATGCT  GTCCAGGCAG  GTAGATGACG  ACCATCAGGG  ACAGCTTCAA
601    CGGCTCTTAC  CAGCCTAACT  TCGATCACTG  GACCGCTGAT  CGTCACGGCG  ATTTATGCCG
661    CACATGGACG  CGTTGCTGGC  GTTTTTCCAT  AGGCTCCGCC  CCCCTGACGA  GCATCACAAA
721    CAAGTCAGAG  GTGGCGAAAC  CCGACAGGAC  TATAAAGATA  CCAGGCGTTT  CCCCCTGGAA
781    GCGCTCTCCT  GTTCCGACCC  TGCCGCTTAC  CGGATACCTG  TCCGCCTTTC  TCCCTTCGGG
841    CTTTCTCAAT  GCTCACGCTG  TAGGTATCTC  AGTTCGGTGT  AGGTCGTTCG  CTCCAAGCTG
901    ACGAACCCCC  CGTTCAGCCC  GACCGCTGCG  CCTTATCCGG  TAACTATCGT  CTTGAGTCCA
961    ACACGACTTA  ACGGGTTGGC  ATGGATTGTA  GGCGCCGCCC  TATACCTTGT  CTGCCTCCCC
1021   GCGGTGCATG  GAGCCGGGCC  ACCTCGACCT  GAATGGAAGC  CGGCGGCACC  TCGCTAACGG
1081   CCAAGAATTG  GAGCCAATCA  ATTCTTGCGG  AGAACTGTGA  ATGCGCAAAC  CAACCCTTGG
1141   CCATCGCGTC  CGCCATCTCC  AGCAGCCGCA  CGCGGCGCAT  CTCGGGCAGC  GTTGGGTCCT
1201   GCGCATGATC  GTGCT       CCTGTCGTTG  AGGACCCGGC  TAGGCTGGCG  GGGTTGCCTT
1281   AGAATGAATC  ACCGATACGC  GAGCGAACGT  GAAGCGACTG  CTGCTGCAAA  ACGTCTGCGA
1341   AACATGAATG  GTCTTCGGTT  TCCGTGTTTC  GTAAAGTCTG  GAAACGCGGA  AGTCAGCGCC
```

'There are about three billion pieces in a whole DNA chain. It would take scientists years to find all the pieces. But these powerful computers do this work.

'The DNA in most animals is quite similar. Only a few pieces are different in different animals. So we look at the pieces of dinosaur DNA. Then we look at the DNA of different animals alive today. We use modern animal DNA to complete the chain.'

'How do you complete the chain?' asked Ellie.

'Look at the screen again,' replied Wu. 'There is a hole in line 1201. The hole shows where we need to repair the dinosaur DNA.

'The computers can check millions of pieces of DNA. They

remember lots of different types of DNA. They will search in their memories and find a piece of a chain which looks the same. Then the computers will go back to that sequence in the chain and put a DNA piece in it.'

Wu pressed some keys on the computer keyboard[54] and immediately the hole in the sequence in line 1201 was filled by more letters.

'I see how you make the dinosaur DNA,' said Grant. 'But how do you know what kind of animal you are making?'

'Oh,' said Wu, 'we just let it grow. We find out what kind of animal it is when it is born. I'll show you.'

Wu took them through a door with a sign saying: FERTIL-IZATION[55]. Then he told them how the dinosaur embryos were put into special eggs. He talked about the special shells of the eggs and the temperature of the room.

Tim was bored. He was more interested when Wu showed them some syringes[56] with poison in them.

'Sometimes we have to inject poison into the eggs and kill the animal if something goes wrong,' Wu said.

Next, Wu took them into a room with a sign on the door saying: HATCHERY[57]. The room was hot and there were rows and rows[58] of eggs lying on shelves.

'This is where the eggs hatch and the dinosaurs are born,' Wu said.

'How many eggs hatch and become living dinosaurs?' asked Gennaro.

'Not many,' said Wu. 'Only about 0.4 per cent of the eggs hatch into living dinosaurs. But we have got 238 live dinosaurs now. Fifteen different species.'

'When are they adults?' Grant asked Wu.

'They are adults in two to four years. We have some full-size adults in the park now. We even have a young tyrannosaur and a full-size adult one,' Wu answered. 'Let's go into the Nursery and we'll find out if there are any new babies.'

The Nursery was a white room. In it there were lots of glass incubators[59]. They looked like the incubators used for small babies in hospitals. In one incubator was a little animal. It was like a lizard, about 30 cm tall. Its skin was dark yellow with brown stripes[60]. It had strong hind legs and it used its straight, thick tail to help it to stand up.

'*Velociraptors*[61] are very fierce when they grow up into adults,' said Wu. 'But at the moment this is just a friendly baby.'

'Two days ago I was digging up a fossilized velociraptor's bones and eggs,' said Grant. 'And here is a live one!'

Grant opened the lid of the incubator to look at the baby dinosaur. And the little animal squeaked[62] and jumped into Tim's arms. Tim held it close to him. Its little tongue moved quickly in and out of its mouth.

'Will it bite me?' asked Tim.

'No, it will be friendly,' said Wu. 'It won't hurt you. And baby raptors don't have egg teeth.'

'What are egg teeth?' asked Nedry. He was bored. He was only interested in going to the computers in the Control Room.

'Well, the babies of most dinosaurs have a little "tooth" on their nose. This helps the dinosaurs to break the shell of their egg when they are born. But we have to help the raptors out of their shells because they don't have egg teeth.'

'What do they do when they breed[63] in the park, then?' asked Grant. 'How do they get out of their eggs in their nests?'

The little animal squeaked and jumped into Tim's arms.

'They don't,' said Wu. 'We don't let the dinosaurs breed. They all come out of the special eggs like the ones which you saw in the Hatchery.'

'How can you stop the dinosaurs in the park from breeding?' asked Malcolm.

'Remember that we make the dinosaurs,' said Wu. 'We can make them what we want them to be. They can't breed in Jurassic Park because we only make female dinosaurs.

'Now, Tim, if you put down your new friend, I will take you all to the Control Room.'

'Tell me, Dr Wu,' said Malcolm, as they walked back to the Control Room, 'is one of the species you have made the ... what was it called, Dr Grant?'

'Compsognathus,' replied Grant.

'Oh, yes, we've made a lot of those,' said Wu. 'Compys are very useful to us. We have found out that the compys eat the droppings[64] of the larger animals. Animals like apatosaurs leave droppings which are ten times larger than elephants' droppings. So we need lots of compys to eat their droppings. There are 50 compys, I think.'

'What if one of the compys escaped ...'

'You're thinking of the animals which have attacked children in Costa Rica,' said Wu. 'They weren't compys. We know where all our animals are. There are sensors and video cameras[65] in the park and the computers count the animals every few minutes. We would know if an animal escaped.'

'Here is the Control Room. I'll show you what Dr Wu means,' said Ed Regis.

They went into the Control Room. Dennis Nedry went to a computer in a corner of the room to start work.

All the video screens were showing the same picture – a

ship. It was beside the main dock in the north of the island.

'That is our supply ship. It has brought us equipment and food,' said Arnold, the chief engineer. 'It comes here every two weeks.'

'We'll show you the park's control systems when they've unloaded the ship,' said Regis.

'Are there any adult raptors in the park, Ed?' Ellie asked Regis. 'Scientists would like to know how they behave. They think that raptors were very fierce animals which hunted in groups. It would be interesting to know if that's true.'

Regis and Wu looked at each other.

'Well,' said Regis slowly, 'there are eight adult raptors but they are in an enclosure behind the Control Centre. They haven't been put into the park yet.'

'Can we see them while we're waiting?' asked Grant.

'Yes. OK,' said Regis. 'If you go out of here and round behind the building you'll find the enclosure. Come back here after you've seen them.'

Ellie, Grant, Malcolm and Tim went to see the raptors. On the way to the raptors' enclosure, they passed a long, low building made of concrete. There was a smell of oil and they could hear a humming sound.

'That's the noise of a very large generator[66],' said Malcolm.

'I guess it's generating electricity for the whole island,' said Grant.

Soon they came to an enclosure with a very strong metal fence around it. The fence was about 4 m high and there was a humming sound. It was a powerful electric fence. Inside the enclosure there was thick vegetation – lots of plants and bushes – about 2 m high. They couldn't see any animals but they could hear footsteps.

'Where are they?' asked Tim.

Then they saw a head. It was a metre long with a long nose and very sharp teeth. The animal's skin was dark yellow with brown stripes. The adult raptor was the same colour as the baby in the Nursery.

The raptor watched them with large, dark eyes. It held the leaves of the plants with its front foot. The foot looked like a hand with three very long, sharp claws.

Suddenly the attack came. Two other raptors ran at the fence and hit it. They hit the fence so hard that the people did not know what was happening. The electric fence made a loud noise and sparks[67] flew up. The animals fell back from the fence but they weren't hurt. They stood up and went back into the vegetation. Five more animals were watching. They made hissing sounds like snakes.

Ellie and Grant, Malcolm and Tim were frightened and shocked.

'Those animals wanted to kill us,' said Malcolm, as they went back to the Control Centre.

'Yes,' said Grant.

'I have heard that lions and tigers have to learn that men are easy to kill,' said Malcolm. 'How have these dinosaurs learnt this lesson? I want to see how the Control Room works now!'

5
—

The Control Room

When they were back in the Control Room, the visitors stared at all the computers and screens. Nedry was still working at his computer and did not listen to them.

'Let me show you how we control Jurassic Park and all the animals,' said John Arnold.

He sat down in front of a keyboard. Next to him was a huge map on a piece of glass. The map showed the whole island. He pressed a key on the keyboard and immediately there were lots of thin blue lines on the map.

'The blue lines show the movements of the young tyrannosaur for the last 24 hours,' he said. 'It's in the south-east of the island, near the lake.'

'Where is the adult tyrannosaur?' asked Gennaro.

Arnold pressed another key and one blue dot appeared instead of the lines. There was a number next to the dot.

'The adult is north-west of the lake,' said Arnold. 'I can show where all 238 animals are.'

He pressed more keys and lots of dots with numbers next to them appeared on the screen.

'How accurate is that system?' asked Malcolm.

'The dots show us very accurately where an animal is,' answered Arnold. 'I'll show you what else we can do. This system makes sure that we can't lose any animal. There are sensors which detect movement and there are video cameras. The computer checks the video pictures and its recognizes the different species of dinosaurs. It counts all the animals in each species every 15 minutes. I'll show you.'

'I can show where all 238 animals are,' said Arnold.

Total Animals	238	
Species	*Expected*	*Found*
Tyrannosaurs	2	2
Maiasaurs	21	21
Stegosaurs	4	4
Triceratops	8	8
Compsognathids	49	49
Othnielia	16	16
Velociraptors	8	8
Apatosaurs	17	17
Hadrosaurs	11	11
Dilophosaurs	7	7
Pterosaurs	6	6
Hypsilophodontids	33	33
Euoplocephalids	16	16
Styracosaurs	18	18
Callovosaurs	22	22
Total	**238**	**238**

'If an animal dies, the computer tells us in a few minutes,' continued Arnold. 'The system shows the number of animals of that species that we put into the park. And it shows the number of live animals that the sensors have found. It can't go wrong.'

'Do you mean there are sensors all over the park?' asked Malcolm.

'Well – there are sensors in 92 per cent of the park. There are a few places we can't put sensors – Jungle River, for example. The movement of the water means that sensors wouldn't work there. But the sensors detect animals going into that sector[68] and tell us if the animals don't appear again.'

'Can the animals get out of their enclosures?' asked Gennaro.

'No,' replied Arnold. 'There is a very good security system. There are deep moats and there are also extremely powerful electric fences.'

'But what would happen if an animal did escape from its enclosure?' asked Gennaro.

It was Muldoon, the park warden, who answered the question. 'We'd catch it. I've got all kinds of tranquillizer guns[69] which will work on different sizes of animals. These won't kill the animals. But they will knock them down and make them sleep. The dinosaurs were very expensive to make. So Mr Hammond doesn't want to hurt them.'

'Mr Arnold, what about the compys?' asked Malcolm. 'Can you find each one of them?'

'Oh, yes. They stay together in two large groups but we can check on all of them. We made three batches[70] of compys and put them into the park at different times.'

'And can your computer give you a report on all of them together?' asked Malcolm.

'Yes, it can.' Arnold pressed more keys on the keyboard. 'For example, this is a graph which shows the heights of all the compys.'

They all looked at the graph on the screen. It showed a line going up in a peak to the middle and then down again.

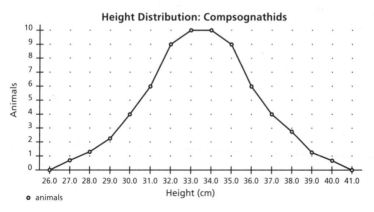

Height Distribution: Compsognathids

Animals / Height (cm)

o animals

'There you are,' said Arnold. 'The graph shows the heights of the compys. A graph of any group of animals would look like this.'

'You don't expect anything unusual on the graphs for the animals in the park?' asked Malcolm.

'No,' replied Arnold.

Malcolm looked worried. But he didn't say anything else.

Then Gennaro spoke. 'Could someone damage the system that runs the park?' he asked.

'No, this system runs on electricity from its own generator,' said Arnold. 'If the main generator stops working, there is an emergency generator. The emergency generator will provide power while we are mending the main one.

'There is really nothing to worry about, Mr Gennaro,' went on Arnold. 'And now it's time to start your tour of the park.'

As they were leaving the Control Room, Gennaro spoke to Malcolm. 'It looks like a good, safe system to me.'

'Things are already going wrong,' replied Malcolm. 'That graph showed the heights of a normal group of animals. And it shouldn't. This is not a normal place and those are not normal animals.'

'I don't understand,' said Gennaro.

'You soon will,' replied Malcolm.

As they left the Control Room, Ed Regis gave each of them – Grant, Malcolm, Gennaro, Ellie and Tim and Lex – a baseball cap. On the front of each cap there was a badge with a picture of a dinosaur and the words: JURASSIC PARK.

They went down the stairs for the start of the tour of the park.

———

Hammond came into the Control Room. He watched through the window as his visitors left the building to go on the tour.

'I hope *they* are amazed by what I've done,' he said to himself. 'Because Arnold and Muldoon and Wu are all complaining about the park now.

'Arnold worries about the behaviour of the animals and it isn't his job to worry about what they do.

'Muldoon isn't happy. He says that some of the animals are too dangerous and we shouldn't let people near them. He's wrong. We just need to find out more about these animals.

'There have been some problems and some accidents with the dinosaurs. A worker was blinded by the poison from a *dilophosaur*[71]. We found out that dilophosaurs can spit[72] their poison 15 m so that an animal is paralyzed. If the visitors to the park keep the windows of their vehicles closed, no one will be hurt.

'Muldoon wants to destroy the raptors. He says they are too dangerous and clever. We know they can open doors and they can jump very high. They have escaped from all the enclosures we've made for them. They hunt together in a group and they like killing things. They've killed three workers. But many zoos have problems like these. We can sort these problems out.

'Perhaps Muldoon will stop worrying now. I've given him a rocket launcher to fire at the animals in an emergency. But only Muldoon and I have keys to the cupboard where it is kept. I don't want my animals harmed.'

Hammond stared out of the window.

'Why aren't people pleased to be working here?' he said to

41

himself. 'I've given Wu the best job a geneticist could ever have. He's worked very hard. In five years he has made living dinosaurs. We always believed that dinosaurs were slow and stupid. But now we know they were not. But Wu says they move too fast and they're too intelligent and too dangerous. Now he wants to change them. He wants to make dinosaurs which are slow and stupid. But I don't want to do that.

'And then there's Nedry over there in the corner,' Hammond thought angrily. 'His company has been paid a huge amount of money to build a computer system to control this island. But the system is still full of bugs. So now he's trying to sort the problems out. He's using all our phone lines for the whole weekend so he can send information back to his main computer in the States.

'And now I've got these visitors. Gennaro is a businessman. If he thinks the park is going to make money he won't make any trouble. Grant and Sattler aren't going to make trouble either. They want to study living dinosaurs. But I don't like Malcolm. I don't like his chaos theory and his predictions of trouble. He says the systems in the park will break down[73] because you can't put animals from millions of years ago into a modern world. He's wrong. This is an animal park – not a complex system. And soon I'll have two more animal parks like this. Jurassic Park Europe and Jurassic Park Japan will be open in four years' time. I'm going to make a lot of money ...'

Hammond left the Control Room.

6

The Tour of the Park

Ed Regis took the visitors to a road which came from a garage under the Control Centre. Immediately, two large vehicles came up from the garage and stopped in front of them. There were no drivers!

'No more than four people in each tour vehicle, please,' said a voice. It came from a loudspeaker[74] on a wall.

'We've got 30 of these land-cruisers[75],' said Regis. 'They run on electricity. They get the electricity from a rail in the road and they cannot leave the main visitors' road. We've also got two petrol vehicles – Jeeps[76] – which we can use if we have to. And there are some big maintenance trucks[77] which we keep about 2 km away. There's a separate road for the Jeeps and the trucks. Dr Harding, the vet, is out in a Jeep now. We'll probably meet him down in the south of the island.'

Gennaro and the three scientists got into the first land-cruiser and Regis got into the second with Lex and Tim. Tim sat in the front seat and looked around the land-cruiser excitedly. He soon found there was a computer inside and a walkie-talkie[78] and a strange-looking pair of goggles.

'We can talk to the Control Room using a radio linked[79] to the computer. We can speak to the other land-cruiser using a walkie-talkie,' said Regis.

'The computer in each vehicle gives full information about everything in the park.' Regis went on. 'The sensors in the park tell the main computer in the Control Room where the land-cruisers are. Then the main computer tells the computers in the land-cruisers what to tell you.'

The land-cruisers slowly started moving.

'Welcome to Jurassic Park,' said the voice of the computer. 'Most dinosaurs were not very big. The first animals we are going to see are the same size as a horse. Look to the left and you will see some *hypsilophodontids*[80].'

The land-cruisers stopped and the children looked out of the windows.

'I can't see anything,' said Lex. 'This is boring.'

'The hypsilophodontids are hiding in the long grass,' said the voice on the computer. 'Let's call them.'

There was a loudspeaker on the fence next to the road. It suddenly made a trumpeting noise. Six strange animals' heads came up out of the grass one after the other. They looked so funny that Lex and Tim laughed.

The land-cruisers moved on. 'If you look down the hill from the road you will see the Jungle River,' said the voice. 'And perhaps you will see the dilophosaurs. When a dilophosaur is hungry, it spits poison at an animal to paralyze it. The animal can't move so the dilophosaur can eat it.'

On the computer screen, Tim saw a picture of an animal which looked like a bird. It had a long neck and yellow and black spots[81] on its body. It had two bright red crests[82] which went from its eyes to its nose in a V-shape. When Tim looked out of the window, he saw the real animal. It was about 3 m tall and it was drinking from the river. The animal made a hooting noise. It sounded like an owl.

'It's pretty,' said Lex.

The next animals Tim saw were the *triceratops*[83]. There were two of them in an enclosure on the right of the road.

They were the same colour as elephants. Each animal had three horns on its head. The horns near their eyes were 2 m long. They had huge crests made of bone behind their heads.

'Triceratops cannot see very well and they weigh about 6 tonnes each,' said the computer's voice.

'They're very boring,' said Lex. 'Why don't they move?' She opened the land-cruiser window. 'Hey, stupid dinosaurs. Move!' she shouted.

Regis quickly closed the window again.

'And now,' said the computer. 'We're going to see the most famous dinosaur of all – tyrannosaurus rex.'

The land-cruisers moved forwards and stopped at the top of a hill. Below them was a large forest. It was the end of the afternoon. The sun was going down and there was mist in the distance. Everywhere it was quiet and peaceful. Was the world like this millions of years ago?

Alan Grant's voice came over the walkie-talkie. 'Tell me about the tyrannosaurs, Ed.'

'Well, we have two tyrannosaurs,' Ed replied. 'One is a young one – about 2 years old. It's 2.50 metres high and weighs about 1.50 tonnes. It's probably down by the lake. The other one is an adult. It's probably hiding among the trees, but it will come out to eat soon.'

The computer started talking about the tyrannosaur, but no one listened. They heard the sound of a frightened animal. Suddenly they saw a goat in the enclosure.

'What's happening? Is the dinosaur going to eat the goat?' Lex was frightened.

'Look. It's here,' said Grant quietly. 'The big tyrannosaur has come. Look.'

The head of the tyrannosaur was 6 m above the ground. It

was huge and square, about 2 m long with red-brown skin. The animal had enormous jaws and teeth.

Suddenly, the tyrannosaur jumped out from behind the trees. It reached the goat in four huge steps and bit it through the neck. There was silence.

'Oh, my God,' said Malcolm quietly. 'It's as big as a house.'

The tyrannosaur looked around.

'It can see us,' said Regis. 'It will take the goat away to eat it.'

But the tyrannosaur started to eat the goat.

'Eww, that's horrible,' said Lex.

Then suddenly the animal picked up the goat and carried it away into the forest.

'Ladies and gentlemen,' said the voice of the computer, 'that was tyrannosaurus rex.' The voice sounded pleased.

'If one of those animals escaped — ,' said Gennaro. 'I don't want to think about it.'

The sky was getting cloudy now and the wind was blowing.

'I think it's going to rain,' said Regis to the children.

The land-cruisers slowly moved on along the road.

'Now you are going to see some *sauropods*[84] – the plant-eating apatosaurs and *hadrosaurs*[85],' said the computer.

Tim looked out of the window of his land-cruiser. He saw long-necked apatosaurs moving gracefully through the trees with some smaller hadrosaurs. Suddenly, he saw a much smaller animal, moving very fast among the trees. It was dark yellow, with brown stripes on its back.

'Look!' Tim shouted. 'There's a young velociraptor!'

'We must go back and check,' said Grant's voice over the walkie-talkie. 'This could be serious.'

'We can't go back,' replied Regis. 'These vehicles can only go forwards.'

'Tim, this is Professor Malcolm,' came another voice. 'How old was the animal you saw?'

'It was older than the baby we saw in the Nursery,' replied Tim. 'But it was smaller than the adults we saw in the raptor enclosure. It was about a metre high.'

'Thanks, Tim,' said Malcolm slowly.

As the land-cruisers went towards the south of the island, the visitors suddenly saw something strange. Next to a Jeep, a man was examining a huge animal. It was about 6 m long with big plates of bone along its back. Along its tail were long spikes[86]. Its head was very small and it looked very stupid. The animal lay quietly while the man examined it.

'It's a *stegosaur*[87],' said Tim.

'That thing is very big,' said Lex, as they all got out of their vehicles and walked towards it. 'And it smells bad,' she added.

'The stegosaur is sick,' said Regis. 'Dr Harding has tranquillized it. That's why it isn't moving.'

'What's wrong with it?' Ellie asked the vet.

'I don't know,' replied Dr Harding. 'They get sick every six weeks and we can't find out why.'

Ellie looked at the animal's eyes and tongue. 'I think it's been poisoned,' she said. 'Perhaps it's been eating those bushes over there. The berries[88] from those bushes are poisonous.'

'I've thought about that,' said Harding. 'So I've watched the stegosaurs carefully. I'm sure they don't eat the bushes.'

Ellie started looking around. She found berries on the ground and she found piles of small round stones.

'I know what's wrong,' Ellie said to Harding. 'These are

47

gizzard stones. Perhaps the stegosaurs use gizzard stones. And when they pick up new gizzard stones from the ground they also eat the berries. They must get poisoned every six weeks when they need new stones.'

'Yes, of course,' said Harding to Ellie. 'Some reptiles don't use their teeth to break up their food. They swallow stones with sharp edges and use them instead. When the stones are smooth and round they spit them out and swallow new ones. Stegosaurs must do the same thing.'

Grant walked across to Ellie. He bent down to look at the stones. Then he picked something up.

'Ellie,' he said quietly, 'look at this.'

Ellie looked at what he was holding. Then she looked worried. Gennaro and Malcolm went over to Ellie and Grant.

'These are pieces of shell from a dinosaur egg,' said Grant. 'The dinosaurs are breeding.' He showed them some small, white pieces of egg-shell.

'I knew they were,' said Malcolm.

'The dinosaurs can't breed,' said Harding.

'Are you sure these are from a dinosaur egg?' Gennaro asked Grant.

'Of course I'm sure,' replied Grant. 'I've seen shells from dinosaurs' eggs before. These are pieces of a shell from a velociraptor's egg!'

'I'll call the Control Room on my radio,' said Harding, and he went back to his Jeep.

They all followed him. Harding spoke to the Control Room. Arnold and Wu were there.

'I don't believe it,' said Arnold, when they told him over the radio.

'The dinosaurs can't breed,' said Wu.

'These are pieces of shell from a dinosaur egg,' said Grant.
'The dinosaurs are breeding.'

'Let's do a test,' said Malcolm. 'Arnold, can you check some information on your computer in the Control Room and show it on the screen in Dr Harding's Jeep?'

'Yes, I can.'

'Right, ask the computer to count all the animals in the park and show us the number on the screen.'

While they waited for the computer to show the number, Malcolm continued speaking.

'I knew that the compys were breeding when Arnold showed us that graph of the heights of the animals. Three batches of compys were put into the park at different times. So a graph should show three peaks. But there was only one peak in the line on the graph – not three. One peak shows that there is one group of compys of lots of different ages and heights. And that means that they are breeding.'

Some information came onto the screen of the computer in the Jeep. The bottom line of the screen showed: Total expected – 238. Total number found – 238.

'Arnold,' said Malcolm, 'ask the computer to look for 239 animals.'

A moment later, the screen changed. The bottom line showed: Total expected – 239. Total number found – 239. The number of compsognathids had gone up by one.

'Now look for 300 animals,' said Malcolm.

The numbers on the screen started to change. They changed and changed. Then the numbers stopped at a total of 292. Everyone stared at the screen. No one said anything.

'You asked the computer to look for the number of animals you had put in the park,' said Malcolm. 'You asked it to find out if any animals had died. You did not ask the computer to find out if there were any more animals.'

Total Animals	292	
Species	*Expected*	*Found*
Tyrannosaurs	2	2
Maiasaurs	21	22
Stegosaurs	4	4
Triceratops	8	8
Compsognathids	49	65
Othnielia	16	23
Velociraptors	8	37
Apatosaurs	17	17
Hadrosaurs	11	11
Dilophosaurs	7	7
Pterosaurs	6	6
Hypsilophodontids	33	34
Euoplocephalids	16	16
Styracosaurs	18	18
Callovosaurs	22	22
Total	**238**	**292**

'As you can see, you've got more *maiasaurs*[89] and hypsilophodontids. You've got a lot more compys and *othnielia*[90]. And you've got 37 raptors instead of 8!'

'We must start looking for the nests,' said Grant. 'We can count broken eggs. Then we can find out if any dinosaurs have escaped from the island.'

'Dr Wu,' Grant said into the radio, 'did you use frog DNA when you repaired the dinosaur DNA?'

'It's possible that I did,' replied Wu. 'But I don't understand what's happening.'

'I do,' said Grant. 'The animals have started to breed.'

7

Death in Jurassic Park

Friday evening: in the park

Harding, Grant, Ellie, Malcolm, Lex, Tim and Gennaro all stood next to Harding's Jeep. The stegosaur lay quietly nearby.

'Can we go back to the Safari Lodge now?' said Lex. 'I'm very hungry.'

'Yes, let's go,' said Grant, smiling at her.

'I'm going to stay here with Dr Harding,' said Ellie. 'I want to examine the stegosaur more closely.'

'I'll stay here too," said Gennaro. 'I'll come back later in the Jeep with Dr Sattler and Dr Harding.'

'I'll come back now, with you,' said Malcolm to Grant.

'OK, let's go,' replied Grant.

'I want to ride in the front land-cruiser with Dr Grant this time,' said Tim.

'You can't, Tim,' said Malcolm. 'Dr Grant and I want to talk to each other.'

'Listen, Tim,' said Regis. 'Dr Grant and Professor Malcolm can ride in the second land-cruiser. You come in the first land-cruiser with Lex and me. You can use the night-vision goggles which you found in the other land-cruiser. They make it easy to see things at night. It's getting dark now. You'll be able to see in the dark while we drive back.'

'Great,' said Tim, and he ran off to get the goggles from the second land-cruiser.

The two groups got into the land-cruisers and the two

electric vehicles started moving. Rain was starting to fall. Soon the road curved round in a circle and the land-cruisers went north back towards the Safari Lodge.

———

Friday evening: Nedry

In the Control Centre, Muldoon was feeling unhappy and worried and he did not know why. The park warden was sure that something was going to go wrong out in the park. He was so worried that he went down to the storeroom under the building. He unlocked the cupboard where he kept the rocket launcher. He took out the launcher and collected some rockets and some tranquillizer canisters.

Then Muldoon took the rocket launcher, the rockets and the canisters to the garage and put them into the back of the second Jeep. He went back upstairs to the Control Room and stared out of the windows. He didn't speak. It was getting dark and rain was pouring down.

Nedry sat quietly in front of his computer screen. He hated Hammond. Hammond wanted more changes to the computer system but he had refused to pay more money. Nedry was angry. So he had been very pleased when the man from Biosyn had offered him a huge amount of money. Nedry was going to steal the frozen dinosaur embryos and Biosyn was going to pay him $1 500 000.

'I'm going to get a drink from the machine downstairs,' said Nedry to the others in the Control Room. 'I won't be long. Don't touch anything.' Then he pressed a key on his keyboard and left.

'I don't like that man,' said Arnold as Nedry left.

The bugs in the computer system were not mistakes. Nedry had programmed the computers wrongly. Now he had pressed a computer key to make the power shut down[91]. In a few minutes all the electric power on the island would shut down except the power in the Control Room. None of the sensors, video cameras, electric fences or door locks would work.

Nedry was going to go to the Fertilization Room. He was going to steal the embryos, then take a Jeep. He was going to drive to the small dock in the east of the island and put the canister of embryos on the boat sent by Biosyn. No one would see him because all the sensors and cameras were turned off. Then he was going to return to the Control Room and turn on the power again. No one would know what he had done. He had ten minutes to steal the embryos. He had ten more minutes to take the embryos to the boat and return to the Control Room. It was a clever plan.

Nedry's plan worked well for the first ten minutes. He pushed open the door marked – FERTILIZATION. He got the canister of shaving foam out of a bag. He found the store of embryos and quickly filled the bottom of the canister with the small glass tubes of embryos. Then he went downstairs to the garage and got into the Jeep. The rocket launcher lay on the back seat.

Nedry smiled to himself. 'This is easy!' he said.

It was dark and the rain was falling heavily. Nedry drove fast. There was thick forest on either side of the road. Where was the east dock? After five minutes, Nedry stopped and jumped out of the Jeep. He was lost!

He ran forward through the darkness and the pouring rain. Where was the east dock? As Nedry ran forward, he heard a hooting sound in the distance.

Is that an owl? he thought.

There was thick vegetation all around him and Nedry did not know where he was. His plan had gone terribly wrong. Soon, people in the Control Centre would ask where he was. He had to go back to the Control Room now. He would try to get the canister to the ship tomorrow night.

As Nedry turned round to go back to the Jeep, he heard the hooting sound again. It was nearer now. A minute later, there was a crashing sound in the forest. Something big was coming towards him! A dinosaur!

Nedry began to run. Suddenly he saw it. It stood 12 m away from him. It was very big – 3 m high, with yellow and black spots and a long neck. It had two bright red crests which went from its eyes to its nose in a V-shape. Nedry knew nothing about dinosaurs. He did not know what it was.

The dinosaur wasn't very close to him. Maybe he could get back to the Jeep. As Nedry started to run again, the dinosaur moved its head back. Nedry felt something hit his chest. He put up his hand and felt something wet. It was horrible. The dinosaur had spat at him!

Nedry tried to get the sticky spit off his chest. Then he realized that his hand was starting to hurt. Suddenly the dinosaur's head moved quickly again and Nedry felt a terrible pain in his eyes. The dinosaur had spat in his eyes! He couldn't see!

The pain was so bad that Nedry fell to the ground. He couldn't move. He could feel the ground shaking as the dinosaur came towards him. His last hope was that this would end soon. It did.

Nedry felt something hit his chest.
The dinosaur had spat at him!

8

The Attack

Friday evening: in the park

It was 7 p.m. and it was still raining heavily. Bright lights shone down on the road. The two land-cruisers suddenly stopped on the road beside the ocean. Grant and Malcolm looked at the first land-cruiser and saw that the children were pointing at a ship. It was the supply ship they had seen on the screens in the Control Room. The ship was going back to Costa Rica.

Grant turned on the walkie-talkie to speak to the first land-cruiser. Lex was speaking excitedly. 'Look! There in the back of the ship. I saw them.'

'What's the problem?' asked Grant.

'The kid says she can see some animals on the supply ship,' replied Regis.

'It's getting dark. How can she see anything?' said Malcolm.

Grant stared at the ship. Yes, in the back of the ship, he could see some dark shapes. Lex was right! The animals were about 60 cm high and stood on their strong hind legs.

'I can see them,' he said.

'Are they compys?' asked Malcolm.

'No,' replied Grant. 'They're young raptors.'

'Oh, God! Velociraptors!' said Regis. 'They're very, very dangerous. They've killed three workmen. And that ship's going to Costa Rica.'

'Call the Control Room,' said Malcolm. 'Tell them to

recall the ship.'

Grant and Malcolm heard crackling[92] noises from the radio.

'There's something wrong with the computer link,' Regis said. 'I can't call the Control Room.'

'Well, we must get back there quickly then,' said Grant. 'How long does it take for the ship to get to Costa Rica?'

'Eighteen hours. It will get there at 11 a.m. tomorrow morning,' replied Regis.

'And how long will it take us to get back to the Control Room?'

'About 15 minutes.'

Regis started the land-cruisers moving again. And then, suddenly, all the lights over the road went out. The land-cruisers slowed and then stopped. There was complete darkness.

'Why have we stopped?' asked Lex.

'I don't know,' said Regis, 'but I'm sure we'll start again in a minute.'

Grant's voice came over the walkie-talkie and Tim picked it up.

'Are you all right?' asked Grant.

'Yes, we're fine,' Tim replied.

'Stay in the vehicle.'

'We will. Don't worry.'

Tim put on the night-vision goggles. When he looked through them, everything was bright green. There was a tall fence next to them. They had stopped on a hill near the tyrannosaurs' enclosure. Perhaps they would see the rex again.

'I'm hungry,' said Lex.

'I know,' replied Regis. 'But there must be something wrong with the electricity. When they've fixed it, the land-cruisers will start moving again.'

There was a sudden crack of thunder and lightning flashed. The rain poured down.

Tim went on looking through his goggles. The rain was making all the tree branches and leaves move. He looked higher and higher – and stopped. He saw the huge head of the adult tyrannosaur. It was looking over the fence at the land-cruisers.

'Tim?' came Grant's voice from the other land-cruiser. 'Have you got the goggles on? Can you see anything?'

'The rex is standing by the fence.'

Tim watched the dinosaur. He looked down from its huge head to its enormous body and small, strong front legs. It was holding onto the fence with one claw.

'Oh God,' said Regis. His body started to shake. He was terrified. The power was off! They were in terrible danger. He had to do something! Anything! And he opened the door, got out and ran. Rain poured into the land-cruiser through the open door.

'He's left us,' said Lex. 'He's left us!' And she started to scream.

'Shut the door!' Tim shouted at her.

Tim looked again at the rex. It was holding onto the fence! The fence wasn't electrified any more!

The huge animal gave a terrible roar.

'Lex, shut the door!' he shouted.

She didn't move. She was terrified.

'What's happening, Tim?' came Grant's voice over the walkie-talkie.

'Regis ran away,' Tim said into his walkie-talkie. 'I think he saw that the electric fence isn't working.'

'Did the boy say that the fence isn't working?' said Malcolm's voice.

Lightning flashed and they saw a huge hind leg of the dinosaur move forwards and crash down on the fence. Tim climbed into the back of his land-cruiser quickly and shut the door.

'Tim and Lex,' said Grant quickly, 'stay in your vehicle. Be quiet. *Don't move.*'

There was another flash of lightning and they saw the rex take another step forward. Now it was standing on the road between the two vehicles. It bent down and its huge, horrible eye looked in at Tim and Lex.

'Tim!' whispered Lex.

'It's OK. I don't think it can see us.'

The eye disappeared and suddenly the tyrannosaur's head crashed down onto the roof of the first land-cruiser. The glass of the windows cracked and the land-cruiser moved backwards and forwards.

'Lex, where are you?' Tim whispered.

He heard a cry and found her under one of the front seats. Then the animal moved round the vehicle. It got hold of the back of the land-cruiser, lifted it up, then dropped it. A huge hind leg kicked the vehicle onto its side. The dinosaur roared and roared.

'Tim!' screamed Lex.

The rex picked up the land-cruiser in its jaws again. The vehicle went up in the air and Lex fell against a door which opened. Tim saw her fall into the mud of the road but he could do nothing. The vehicle was going round and round in

*Now the tyrannosaur was standing on the road
between the two vehicles.*

the air with him inside it. And then it fell from the dinosaur's jaws, crashed and stopped moving.

———

In the second land-cruiser, Grant and Malcolm heard the noise of the tyrannosaur's attack but they couldn't see anything. The rain ran down the windows of their vehicle. Then the lightning flashed again.

'What's happened to the other land-cruiser? It's gone!' said Malcolm. He sounded terrified. 'What are we going to do now?'

Suddenly Grant could see the dark shape of the dinosaur coming through the rain towards them.

'I don't know what we're going to do,' he said.

Malcolm opened the door of the second land-cruiser and ran. But he was too late. As the lightning flashed again, Grant saw the tyrannosaur jump forwards. It bent its head down and threw Malcolm into the air.

Grant got out of the land-cruiser too. He was starting to run away when the rex turned towards him. Grant stood very still next to the land-cruiser. The rex was only 2 m away. It roared. Its head moved from side to side. Why didn't it attack him? The animal came closer and closer. It knew someone was there. Then Grant realized. It couldn't see him! If he didn't move, the dinosaur couldn't see him!

At last, the angry animal lifted a hind leg and kicked the land-cruiser. The vehicle turned over and over. Grant was hit by the land-cruiser and flew through the air. The vehicle landed with a crash on the ground.

———

Tim opened his eyes. He was lying against one of the doors of his land-cruiser. And the vehicle was moving backwards and forwards. What had happened? Slowly he turned round and looked out of the window. He was in a tree 6 m above the ground! A branch broke and the land-cruiser moved in the tree.

Tim knew that he had to get out before the vehicle fell down from the tree. Carefully, he moved to the door in the back of the land-cruiser. He opened it and climbed out. His feet touched a branch and he began to climb down the tree. Just before he reached the ground, there was a loud cracking noise and the land-cruiser fell. Tim jumped and landed on the soft, wet ground and the vehicle fell beside him.

It was so dark that Tim couldn't see anything. Then he remembered the goggles. He found them in the wreck[93] of his land-cruiser and put them on. Tim and the land-cruiser had fallen onto soft ground below the road.

Tim couldn't see anyone. He was very frightened. He wanted to cry.

'Lex!' he shouted. 'Lex!'

He listened. Then he shouted again. At last, he heard someone shout back.

He found his sister hiding in a big pipe under the road. She was crying.

'Lex, it's me. Come out.'

'No. There's animals out there.'

'It's OK. They've gone.'

'There's a big one.'

'It's all right, Lex. The rex has gone.'

'Where's Dr Grant?' Lex asked.

'I don't know.'

'Dr Grant? Hello! Dr Grant!' she shouted.

Tim was worried that the tyrannosaur might hear the

shouts. But a minute later, he heard another shout. Through his goggles, Tim saw Dr Grant climbing down towards them.

'Thank God,' said Grant. 'I've been looking for you.'

They were all wet and dirty but none of them was badly hurt.

'I'm hungry,' said Lex.

'Me too,' said Grant. 'We've got to get back to the Control Room. And we've got to tell them about the raptors on the ship.'

Suddenly they heard someone cough[94]. The noise came from the road above them. They all climbed up to the road. The moon was shining brightly now and they could see Ed Regis. He was standing very still, close to a tree. Was he hiding from something?

Then there was the sound of breathing. Grant made Lex and Tim stand still.

A large, dark shape moved out of the trees. It was the young tyrannosaur and it went past Regis without stopping. It hadn't seen him. Soon the rex had disappeared. Regis moved away from the tree and walked into the middle of the road. He was safe.

Then suddenly, the tyrannosaur attacked. It came out of the trees on the left side of the road and knocked Regis to the ground. Regis stood up and shouted, 'Get away! Get away!'

The dinosaur stepped backwards, then it knocked Regis to the ground again.

It's a young animal, thought Grant. It's playing a game with him!

'Get away!' shouted Regis again, waving his arms.

The tyrannosaur bent down, opening its jaws. Regis began to scream. Then the screaming suddenly stopped. When the dinosaur lifted its head, it was holding Regis. Blood was dripping down from its jaws.

Grant got hold of the children and made them run. They ran and ran until Lex stopped.

'I can't run any more,' she said.

'OK,' said Grant and he picked her up. Grant and Tim went on walking. Soon Lex was asleep. Her head was on Grant's shoulder. Grant tried to remember the big map of the park in the Control Room.

'Dr Grant,' said Tim as they walked, 'I think we are in the tyrannosaurs' enclosure.'

'I think you're right, Tim. I want to find the sensors and read the numbers on them. Then we can find the way out. There are higher numbers in the centre of the enclosure and lower ones at the edges.'

In the forest, they found some sensors. They were green metal boxes on trees. Grant waved his hands in front of each sensor. None of the red lights came on. None of the sensors was working.

They passed sensor number T/S/04, then T/S/03, T/S/02 and T/S/01.

'Are we going to walk all night?' asked Tim.

'No, we can't do that,' replied Grant. 'Let's find somewhere safe and sleep for a few hours. It's 15 hours before the ship gets to Costa Rica. We can get back to the Control Room in the morning and we can recall the ship.'

A few minutes later, they reached a fence. On the other side of the fence was a deep moat, then a big field.

'I think we've reached the sauropods' enclosure,' Grant said.

In the field, he could see a building. He hoped they would

be safe there.

Lex lifted her head from Grant's shoulder.

'Good, you're awake,' he said. 'Can you walk now? The power's still off so we can climb over the fence.'

Grant and the children had to go into the moat on the other side of the fence. The water was cold and dirty. Grant found a way up the steep side of the moat and helped the children to climb out.

The building in the field was a shed filled with hay – food for the animals. One side of the shed was made of thick metal bars.

'Come on,' said Lex and she went in between the bars. Grant and Tim followed her. Grant pushed together some hay on the floor. The children lay down on the hay and went to sleep. Then Grant lay down and he slept too.

9

Power Off

Friday evening

At the same time as the power failed in the park, all the screens went off in the Control Room. Muldoon, Arnold, Wu and Hammond saw the screens go dark.

'What's happened?' asked Muldoon.

'I don't know,' Arnold replied. 'The computers are working in here but all the power in the park has failed. Nothing's working. All the lights, electric fences, sensors and cameras are off.'

'What about the land-cruisers?' asked Wu.

'They've stopped somewhere near the tyrannosaurs' enclosure. The radio link isn't working and I can't use a walkie-talkie to speak to the land-cruisers. They're too far away. We need Nedry. Where is he?'

'I'll go and look for him,' said Wu, and he ran out of the room.

'If the power for the fences is off, the animals can get out,' said Muldoon. 'Harding is OK. He's got a Jeep. But I'm going to take the other Jeep and find the people in the land-cruisers. I don't want any trouble.'

Muldoon left the Control Room. Arnold sat in front of a screen and pressed keys on a keyboard. What was wrong? What had Nedry done to the system?

Outside the Control Room, thunder roared and lightning flashed. The storm was getting worse.

Muldoon ran back into the room. 'The Jeep's gone!' he said. 'Where's Harding and the other Jeep?'

'At the south end of the island. I'll try to speak to Harding on a walkie-talkie,' said Arnold.

'Why don't you take one of the maintenance trucks and look for the land-cruisers?' asked Hammond.

'The trucks are 2 km away in the maintenance building,' said Muldoon. 'The electric fences aren't working. So it isn't safe to walk in the park.'

'I want my grandchildren back here, Muldoon!' shouted Hammond. 'Go and find them!'

Muldoon didn't answer.

'I've spoken to Harding on a walkie-talkie,' said Arnold. 'He and Gennaro and Dr Sattler are only about a kilometre away. They'll be here soon.'

Wu came back into the Control Room. 'Nedry's gone,' he said. 'I can't find him anywhere in the building. And someone has been in the Fertilization Room. One of each of the embryos has gone.'

The men suddenly understood what had happened. The Jeep and the embryos and Nedry had gone. So the computer failure had not been an accident. Nedry had turned the power off so he could steal the embryos. They knew that another company would pay a lot of money for the embryos.

'I'm going downstairs to wait for Harding,' said Muldoon. 'I'll take the Jeep as soon as he returns. And I'll drive over to the maintenance building. I'll send some workmen with trucks to check the animals and the fences. Then I'll go and find the land-cruisers.'

He left and Hammond started shouting again. 'Get this park under control, now, Arnold!'

'Go to the café and get a cup of coffee, Mr Hammond,' said Arnold. 'I'll call you when Muldoon gets back.'

Hammond left the room angrily and Arnold started pressing keys on the keyboard in front of him. Hundreds of lines of numbers and letters appeared.

'What are you doing?' asked Wu.

'I'm checking the whole computer program,' replied Arnold. 'I have to find out what Nedry did to shut off the power.'

He stared at the screen.

'I checked the records in the Fertilization Department,' said Wu. 'Grant was right. I did use frog DNA to repair the dinosaur DNA. There is frog DNA in some of the dinosaurs that we made. But I still don't understand why the dinosaurs are breeding.'

68

Saturday morning

At midnight, Muldoon and Gennaro came into the Control Room. The power was still off. Arnold was still sitting in front of his keyboard. Hammond was back in the room again.

'We've been out on the tour road in the Jeep,' said Muldoon. 'We found Regis and Malcolm near the tyrannosaurs' enclosure. Regis is dead. Malcolm is badly hurt. The big rex attacked them. Ellie and Harding have taken Malcolm to the Safari Lodge. Harding's going to give Malcolm some morphine[95], but he needs to go to hospital. We need a phone line so we can call a helicopter from Costa Rica. Harding thinks Malcolm will die if we don't get him to a hospital.'

'What about Grant and the kids?' asked Arnold.

'Malcolm says Grant, Tim and Lex were there when the rex attacked. But we can't find them. And we think the rex is in the sauropods' enclosure,' said Gennaro.

'You must go out and get the rex,' Hammond said to Muldoon. 'It will kill the other animals.'

Hammond was more worried about his dinosaurs than he was about his grandchildren!

'I'm not going to look for the rex in the dark,' replied Muldoon. 'The rocket launcher is in the back of the Jeep that Nedry took. There's nothing else which will stop a rex. I'll go and check on the other animals.'

'I'll come with you,' said Gennaro.

Arnold had been working for many hours now. He drank coffee and stared at the screens. Nedry had written new commands[96] for the program and had secretly put them into the computer. He had also used all the phone lines to link the system to his computers in the USA. Arnold could not find the command to change the computer program again. Wu did not know how to help him.

But at 5 a.m. on Saturday morning, when Muldoon and Gennaro came into the Control Room again, John Arnold suddenly shouted. 'I've found it!'

'What?' asked Gennaro.

Arnold pointed to the lines of numbers and letters on his computer screen.

'I've found the command to return the system to normal. Nedry wrote commands that would shut off the systems. When Nedry had got what he wanted the program was going to remove all his secret commands. If he had got back, we would never have known about what he did.'

Arnold pressed some keys. Outside, the big lights came on.

'Are the electric fences working now?' asked Muldoon.

'Yes,' said Arnold, 'and the sensors. Everything's working.'

'Phone for a helicopter to get Malcolm to hospital,' said Gennaro.

But the phones still wouldn't work and all Nedry's secret commands had gone from the system.

'There's no way I can find out what's wrong,' said Arnold.

'Why don't you shut the whole system down and start it up again?' asked Wu. 'Then everything will be reset[97].'

Arnold shut down the computer system and restarted it. A minute later, he was talking to someone at a hospital in Costa Rica.

Arnold sat back in his chair. 'A helicopter will come as soon as possible. However the storm is very bad and they can't fly yet. Everything's OK now,' he said. 'Professor

Malcolm's predictions aren't going to come true.'

'What do you mean?' asked Gennaro.

'Professor Malcolm says that after one problem there is always another and another and another. He says that whole systems go out of control and no one ever gets them back under control again. But that is not happening here in Jurassic Park.'

10

The Chase Through the Forest

When Grant woke up on Saturday it was 5 a.m. and it was light. There were now only 6 hours before the ship reached Costa Rica.

He could hear Tim and Lex laughing. He found them touching a baby triceratops though the bars at the front of the shed.

'Isn't it nice?' said Lex happily. 'Do you want to touch it?'

Grant smiled and then looked around. He saw a metal box on a wall labelled: SAUROPOD MAINTENANCE BUILDING. Inside the box was a phone. But when Grant tried to use it, it didn't work.

'I'm going into the park to try to find a sensor,' Grant said to the children. 'Perhaps they are working now. If I set one off then the people in the Control Room will know where we are. Then they'll come and get us. Wait here for me.'

'No – don't leave us,' said Lex.

'OK, then. Come with me,' said Grant.

'Isn't it nice?' said Lex happily. 'Do you want to touch it?'

They went through the bars and started to walk. It was a lovely day. The sky was pink and purple and there was white mist close to the ground. They stopped to watch a group of hadrosaurs eating leaves from the trees beside the lake. Soon afterwards they reached a sensor. Grant waved his hands in front of it but its red light didn't come on. It wasn't working.

'We'll try the next one,' said Grant, pointing across the field.

As they walked, they heard the roar of an animal. The hadrosaurs by the lake were suddenly worried. They started to run and cry out in fear. Then, with a terrible roar, the adult rex ran out of the trees by the lake. It chased the hadrosaurs. Grant and Lex and Tim ran towards some rocks and started to climb them. The ground shook. The huge, 5 tonne hadrosaurs ran round them, crashing and trumpeting.

Grant waited till the hadrosaurs had run past. Then he made the children climb the nearest tree. They could hide there until he was sure the tyrannosaur had gone.

———

Grant waited until everything was quiet again. After an hour he said, 'We must go.'

'No, I won't go,' said Lex. 'I'm not walking out there any more.'

'We have to, Lex.'

'Why?'

'Because its 7 a.m. now and we have to get back to the Control Room and tell them about the ship.'

'Why don't we go on the river? It's close to here,' said Tim. 'And there was a box in the shed we slept in. The label on the box said: INFLATABLE RAFT[98]. We can use the raft to go down the river.'

It was a good idea. It would be safer to travel on the river and faster too.

In the shed, Grant and the children found some useful things. There was an inflatable raft, as Tim had said, and there was a gas cylinder to put air into the raft. There was a map of the island which showed that the river went close to the Control Centre. The map also showed a tunnel which went from the maintenance shed to a small jetty[99] by the lake. The last things they found were a tranquillizer gun and some tranquillizer darts.

'I hope it's a big, safe raft,' said Lex, 'because I can't swim.'

Grant picked up the folded raft and carried it on his shoulders. Then he found the tunnel which went from the shed to the jetty. As they reached the end of the tunnel, they heard strange noises – snorting and buzzing[100] sounds. When they came out of the tunnel, they saw what was making the noise and stood very still. Twenty metres away, the adult rex was asleep under a tree. Blood was dripping from its jaws and a million flies were buzzing around the half-eaten body of a hadrosaur.

Grant waved one hand to tell the children not to move. Quietly, he went to the jetty and unfolded the raft. Then he made the gas cylinder inflate it. There was a loud hissing noise as the air went into the raft. The tyrannosaur snorted and moved, but it did not wake up. Grant slowly put the inflated raft into the water.

The children ran forward and the three of them got into the raft as quietly as they could. Grant pushed the raft away from the jetty and it moved silently out into the lake. Suddenly, Lex put her hands over her mouth and looked very frightened. Noises came from her mouth. She wanted to cough.

'No, Lex,' whispered Tim angrily.

But Lex coughed. Grant got hold of the oars and rowed[101] as fast as he could into the middle of the lake. They looked back to the shore and saw that the rex had woken up.

'I'm sorry,' said Lex. 'I couldn't help it. But anyway, it's OK. The dinosaur can't swim.'

'Of course it can swim, you idiot!' shouted Tim, as the rex stepped into the water. 'Don't you read any books? Everyone knows dinosaurs can swim.'

As the tyrannosaur got closer and closer to the raft, Grant picked up the tranquillizer gun. The animal's huge head went under the raft. It lifted the raft into the air and then splashed it down into the water. Grant fired a dart as the dinosaur's head appeared next to them. The dart hit the side of the animal's face. The rex roared, opening its huge mouth. It was going to eat them!

There was suddenly another roar and they looked back to the shore of the lake. The young rex had found the body of the hadrosaur and was starting to eat it. The adult rex saw what the young animal was doing. It roared, turned away from the raft and swam to the shore. The young tyrannosaur ran away with a piece of meat hanging from its mouth. The adult chased after it and soon they had both disappeared.

Grant stopped rowing.

'Why aren't you rowing, Dr Grant?' asked Lex.

'I'm tired,' he said.

'Then why are we still moving?' asked Tim.

'There must be a strong current in this river. It's moving the raft.'

They were moving north to where the lake went into a

narrow river. And they were moving in the direction of the Control Centre.

The raft moved into the narrow river. The branches of tall trees on either side of the river grew out over the water. Little yellow dinosaurs were jumping in the branches.

'They are *microceratops*[102],' said Tim.

Suddenly there were screams from the microceratops in the trees. The huge head of the adult tyrannosaur came through the trees. Its jaws snapped at the raft and Lex and Tim screamed in terror. But the tall trees were too close together and the dinosaur's body could not get through them. After a few minutes, the rex stopped trying to reach the raft and it moved away.

The raft went on. Grant and the two children were tired and silent. Grant was very worried, but he said nothing. It was 9 a.m. now. They did not have much time left. They must get to the Control Room and contact the supply ship.

'Listen,' said Lex.

In the distance, they heard strange, hooting cries.

'I don't know what's doing that,' said Grant.

'It sounds like owls,' said Tim.

The raft went round a bend in the river. Two dinosaurs were standing on the river bank. They were 3 m tall and had yellow and black spots on their bodies. There were two red crests on their heads.

'Dilophosaurs,' said Grant.

'Are those the ones that spit poison?' asked Lex.

'Yes,' said Tim.

The dilophosaurs were hooting and drinking from the river. Grant put out his arm and caught hold of the branch of a tree. He stopped the raft next to the bank before it went

Suddenly there were screams from the microceratops. The huge head of the tyrannosaur came through the trees.

too close to the dilophosaurs. How were they going to get past these animals? He looked at his watch. It was 9.20.

Suddenly, Grant saw two things. The two dinosaurs were not the same as each other – one was smaller and the colour of its skin was different. And they were behaving strangely – drinking and hooting and looking at each other. The dilophosaurs were a male and a female! And Grant realized that the dinosaurs were watching each other, not the raft.

'Lie down in the bottom of the raft,' he said quickly to the children. 'Don't move and don't say anything.'

He pushed the raft away from the bank of the river. It moved towards the dilophosaurs. No one moved, no one spoke and they held their breath. The raft went quietly past the two animals and on down the river.

11

The Tyrannosaur Again

In the park: Muldoon and Gennaro

At 8 a.m. on Saturday, Muldoon, Arnold, Wu and Hammond were in the Control Room. The power was on. The fences in the park had been mended and most of the animals had been found. But the tyrannosaurs were still free. The blue lines on the map in the Control Room showed that they were in the sauropods' enclosure.

Muldoon was worried – especially about the adult rex. No one had ever tranquillized it. No one had ever been near it!

'What are you going to do about the rex?' asked Hammond. 'I don't want it killing all the sauropods. And I don't want you killing it with a rocket either.'

'I can't use a rocket,' replied Muldoon. 'Nedry took the Jeep with the rocket launcher in it.'

Muldoon was getting angry with Hammond. He decided to go out and look for the adult rex. As he went to get the Jeep he met Gennaro.

'Do you want to do something dangerous?' Muldoon asked. 'I'm going to find the big rex.'

Gennaro didn't want to go with Muldoon, but he couldn't say no. Ten minutes later, he was in the Jeep and they were driving towards the sauropods' enclosure. The radio was on so they could speak to Arnold in the Control Room. Arnold could look at the map and tell them where the rex was.

'How dangerous is this going to be?' asked Gennaro unhappily.

'I've got a tranquillizer gun,' replied Muldoon. 'The tranquillizer darts work on animals which weigh 250 kg. The big rex weighs 8 tonnes.'

'Isn't there anything else you can use?' asked Gennaro.

'Yes – there are some large tranquillizers for the rocket launcher. But the rocker launcher, the rockets and the tranquillizers for the launcher are in the other Jeep. And Nedry took that. So unless we find the other Jeep ...'

'Well, we're in a Jeep,' said Gennaro. 'If the rex comes, we can drive away.'

'The rex can move much faster than a Jeep,' replied Muldoon quietly.

Then the radio came on and they heard Arnold's voice. 'I can't find the big rex now,' he said. 'It isn't showing on any of

the sensors, so it must be down by the river. I can't find
Grant and the kids either. But I've found Nedry. I can see his
Jeep in sector 1104.'

'OK,' said Muldoon. 'We'll go and find him.'

A few minutes later, they reached sector 1104 and stopped
beside the other Jeep. A group of little green compys ran
away as Muldoon and Gennaro arrived. They saw Nedry's
body lying on the ground. The little animals had been eating
it.

'Did the compys kill him?' asked Gennaro.

'No,' replied Muldoon. 'Look at that sticky spit on his
shirt and face. A dilophosaur spat poison at him and paralyzed him. But the rocket launcher, the rockets and the tranquillizers are still in Nedry's Jeep. Let's get them and get
moving again.'

'What about him?' asked Gennaro, pointing at Nedry's
body.

'Leave him there. He tried to steal the embryos,' said
Muldoon. 'It was his own fault. Come on, we've got things to
do.'

Gennaro looked back at Nedry as they drove off. He saw
that the compys had returned to finish their meal.

Five minutes later, Arnold's voice came over the radio
again. 'I've found the big rex. It's very near where you are
now.'

A few moments later, they heard a roar and knew that
Arnold was right. Then they saw the rex. It was about 50 m
away. But it did not see them. It was pushing at the trees and
trying to get through them.

Muldoon stopped the Jeep and picked up the rocket
launcher.

'I'll use one of the large tranquillizer darts,' he said.

He showed Gennaro the huge metal canister. It had a big needle at one end and a heavy weight at the other.

'The weight will make the needle go into the rex's body,' he explained. Then he put the canister into the rocket launcher.

'Get ready to drive away as soon as I tell you,' said Muldoon.

He lifted up the big launcher and pointed it at the rex. He aimed the launcher and fired. But he did not hit the animal.

Muldoon put another canister into the launcher. He aimed again and the rex turned its head. It gave a terrible roar and charged towards them. Muldoon stood still and fired again. This time the needle went into the rex's skin. But the animal did not fall to the ground. The tranquillizer was not working. The rex continued to run towards the men.

Muldoon ran to the Jeep and jumped in. 'Go! Go!' he shouted.

Gennaro drove off as fast as he could towards some trees. When he reached them, the rex gave one more terrible roar and stopped chasing them.

'I'm sure I hit it that time,' said Muldoon. 'One of those tranquillizers can't be big enough. We'll have to go back for some more canisters.'

They drove back to the Safari Lodge.

———

In the park: Grant, Tim and Lex

On the Jungle River, the raft was moving very quickly. Grant was pleased that they were getting closer to the Control Centre. They would be safe there. But he was still worried that no one knew where they were.

Suddenly they heard a loud sound. The raft started moving faster and faster.

'What's that noise?' asked Tim.

'I think it's a waterfall[103],' said Grant.

They saw a line on the water where the river seemed to end. Grant used the oars and tried to stop the raft but it just went round in a circle. The noise of the water got louder.

Lex was terrified. 'I can't swim!' she shouted.

One of Grant's oars hit a rock and the raft stopped suddenly on the edge of the waterfall. The water fell straight down for 20 m. And there, in the pool at the bottom of the waterfall, was the big rex!

The current was too strong. Grant couldn't hold the raft and it fell over the waterfall. The three of them fell too – down and down and down.

Grant fell into the cold water first. It carried him past the huge hind leg of the tyrannosaur. Then he began to swim towards the edge of the pool. Suddenly he saw Tim. He caught the boy as he was carried past him. But where was Lex?

Next to the dinosaur's horrible tail, Grant saw the little girl. Her face was in the water and she wasn't moving. Grant went under the water again and swam towards her. He caught her arm and he pulled her out onto the edge of the pool. Lex coughed and water came out of her mouth. Tim started to cry but Lex opened her eyes and smiled.

'Thank God, you're OK,' said Grant. 'Now, come on. We must find somewhere to hide.'

Near the waterfall, the rex was moving its head backwards and forwards in the water. It was looking for them in the pool.

Grant saw a path that went up next to the waterfall. Perhaps they would be safer up there. Very quietly, he led the children up the path. He saw that the path disappeared behind the waterfall! Soon they were on a small ledge[104] behind the water. There were metal pipes and noises from electrical machinery. And there was a metal door in a concrete wall.

'What is this place?' asked Lex.

'It's part of the park,' replied Grant. 'They made this waterfall when they made Jurassic Park.'

On the wall, Grant found a keypad[105]. There were some numbers written on the wall next to the keypad. He pressed the same numbers on the keypad. Quietly, the door opened. On the wall inside there was an arrow and the words: MAINTENANCE VEHICLE. The arrow pointed along a tunnel.

Grant went through the door. But before he could stop it, the door closed behind him. Grant couldn't find a keypad or a handle on his side of the door. He hoped Tim would open the door again quickly.

It was very dark in the tunnel. Grant got the tranquillizer gun out of his pocket. Then he started to move forwards with one hand on the wall. His hand found something on a small ledge on the wall. A torch! He picked it up, pressed the switch and its light came on. Ahead of him, Grant saw a small electric car – the maintenance vehicle. He also saw that he was in a long, straight tunnel. He had found the way out!

Grant turned to go back for the children. At that moment, there was a hissing noise behind him. He turned round quickly as a small animal jumped at him. As he lifted the tranquillizer gun and fired, the animal knocked him to the ground. It lay on top of him without moving.

Grant moved the animal, stood up and shone the torch on it. A young velociraptor! It was about 60 cm tall and it was male! Grant left it on the ground and hurried back to the door.

The children had not opened the door because they had another problem. Lex and Tim were standing very still on the ledge behind the waterfall. They were looking at the huge head of the tyrannosaur. It had pushed its nose through the falling water and it was hunting for them.

'It knows we're here,' whispered Tim. 'But it can't see us if we don't move.'

Slowly, a thick, black tongue came out of the animal's mouth. The tongue moved carefully along the ledge.

'Don't move — ' whispered Tim.

But the tongue found him. It wrapped itself around Tim's body, then his head. The rex started to pull the boy towards its mouth.

Lex screamed, 'Tim! Tim!'

She tried to pull her brother back. But she wasn't strong enough.

Then suddenly the tongue let go of Tim. The dinosaur's head fell backwards. It's jaws shut. Then the rex disappeared.

————

In the Control Room

Muldoon and Gennaro were back in the Control Room with Arnold and Wu. The computer was searching for the big rex. The men didn't know where Grant and the children were. Had the rex caught them?

A picture appeared on one of the video screens.

'Look,' said Arnold. 'We've found the big rex.'

The rex started to pull the boy towards its mouth.

The cameras showed the rex standing in the pool at the bottom of the waterfall. Its head was in the waterfall and it looked very strange. Then, very slowly, the tyrannosaur fell. The animal lay on its side in the pool.

'I *did* hit it with that tranquillizer,' said Muldoon. 'It took a long time to work, but I did hit it with the second dart!'

'Good,' said Arnold. 'Malcolm was wrong. Everything is fine. We are in control of the park again.'

'Are we?' asked Gennaro, pointing to a screen behind Arnold. 'Look.'

A message on the screen said: EMERGENCY POWER LOW.

'Why are you using emergency power? Why aren't you using the main power supply?' asked Gennaro.

'Quickly! Print out the information and instructions about the power supply,' said Wu.

Arnold pressed some computer keys. Then Wu collected the printout[106] from the printer. The message on the screen changed. It now said: EMERGENCY POWER FAILURE.

All the computer screens went dark and all the lights went out. Wu went over to a window so he could read the computer printout.

'You shut down the main power supply at 5.13 a.m. You started up the power again at 5.14. But you used the emergency power supply. Now that supply has finished.'

'Oh, God,' cried Arnold. 'We have never shut off the main power supply before. I didn't start it up again properly!'

Wu continued to read the piece of paper. 'You need to start up the main power supply by switching on the main generator,' he said. 'If you start up the power supply by using the computer, you are only using emergency power.'

'Well, I'll go to the generator building and start everything up properly now,' said Arnold. He went to the door.

'Wait,' said Wu, reading the printout. 'There's another problem.'

'What do you mean?' asked Gennaro.

'The emergency power does not run the electric fences,' said Wu. 'It is now about 10 a.m. Since 5.13 a.m. the electric fences haven't been working.'

'And the generator building ...?' asked Gennaro

'... is next to the enclosure where the raptors are kept,' said Wu. 'Or where the raptors were kept, I guess.'

'So you are back in control of the park, are you?' said Gennaro angrily.

_____

In the park: Grant, Tim and Lex

Tim and Lex were sitting on the ledge behind the waterfall. They were breathing very fast. Tim had horrible sticky spit from the tyrannosaur's tongue on his face. He was trying to get it off.

Suddenly, the door opened and Grant came back.

'Did you open the door, Tim?' asked Grant.

'No.'

'The power must be off again,' said Grant.

Slowly and carefully, they walked to the top of the path and looked down into the pool. The tyrannosaur was lying on its side in the water.

'I hope it dies,' said Lex. 'It tried to eat Tim.'

'Come on,' said Grant. 'I've found a tunnel and an electric car which uses a battery. We can get back to the Control Centre. It's 10.15. We've got 45 minutes to get back and recall the supply ship.'

They picked up the young raptor from the tunnel. 'We

must take this back with us,' said Grant.

'Why?' asked Tim.

'Because it's a male animal, Tim. The scientists only made females. So this will prove that the dinosaurs are breeding in the park.'

Grant started the electric car and drove as fast as he could along the tunnel towards the Control Centre.

12

The Battle With the Raptors

In the generator building

'I'm going to the generator building to switch the main power back on,' said Arnold. 'We can't get all the park systems working again if the main electricity supply isn't switched on.'

'The electric fences have been off for 5 hours, so the raptors will be out of their enclosure,' said Muldoon. 'I'll come with you. Unfortunately we've only got 6 rockets for the rocket launcher and there are 8 raptors.'

He turned towards Gennaro. 'Do you want to do something dangerous again?'

'I'll come,' said Gennaro.

'We'll take walkie-talkies,' said Muldoon. 'Go to the Safari Lodge,' he said to Mr Hammond, 'and stay there till we call you.'

Outside the building there were three raptors. Muldoon aimed the launcher at one of the animals and fired. As

Arnold ran to the generator building the rocket exploded and killed the raptor. Muldoon put another rocket into the launcher as the two other raptors got ready to attack him and Gennaro. But it was too late to fire. Muldoon turned and ran. But as he ran he fell down and felt a terrible pain in his foot. He pulled himself into a large pipe under the road. A raptor had followed him and he fired at it. He injured one of its front legs and it ran away, screaming.

Gennaro ran away from Muldoon towards some trees.

It was very dark in the generator building and Arnold left the door open so he could see where he was going. Then he went towards the generator. But suddenly it was dark again. Arnold looked back to the doorway. A raptor stood there. Arnold could not escape. When the raptor left the building a few minutes later, something was hanging from its jaws.

Muldoon spoke to Wu on the walkie-talkie. 'Has Arnold got to the main generator? Is the power on?'

'No, there must be something wrong,' replied Wu. 'And where's Gennaro?'

'I'm in the trees behind the generator building,' said Gennaro's voice. 'I'll go inside now. Wish me luck[107].'

Gennaro did not see any raptors as he went towards the building. But, as he walked into the dark building, he heard a hiss above his head. There, lying on some pipes, was a raptor. Something dark and sticky was dripping from it. Blood!

The animal jumped down onto Gennaro. But he was a strong man and he threw the animal off him. It fell to the ground and Gennaro could see it was hurt. One of its front legs was badly injured. The raptor did not attack again. It slowly walked backwards away from him. Perhaps Gennaro

Muldoon put another rocket into the launcher as the two other raptors got ready to attack.

could now get to the generator. But there were more terrifying noises and Gennaro was a frightened man.

————

In the Safari Lodge

Hammond was sitting next to Malcolm's bed. The mathematician had been very badly injured by the rex. Ellie and Harding had given him morphine. But Malcolm was in great pain. They all knew he would die if he was not taken to hospital soon.

'I told you that things would go wrong,' Malcolm said, 'This is a disaster[108].'

'There was a time when a problem like this couldn't have happened,' he continued. 'Scientists worked slowly and carefully. They learnt to be careful and make sensible decisions. Now anyone can buy powerful scientific knowledge and use it quickly and easily. And look at the disaster you have caused.'

'I only wanted to make an animal park,' said Hammond.

'You wanted to make money,' said Malcolm. 'And disasters happen if people want to get rich by using science ... Don't you understand? It's possible that none of you will leave this island alive.'

'We can't get away until we get help,' said Hammond. 'But the animals can't get away either. So your predictions were wrong. The animals cannot escape. The world is not in danger.'

'The Earth is four and a half BILLION years old,' said Malcolm. 'It has survived many disasters. It will survive what Man does to it. It will survive longer than Man. We don't have the power to destroy the Earth or to save it. But can we save ourselves?' Malcolm smiled. And then he died quietly.

In the Visitors' Centre

The electric car carried Grant, Lex and Tim along the tunnel and stopped near the Visitors' Centre. All the windows of the Centre were broken and the door locks were broken too. A security guard[109] was lying dead on the ground.

Grant took the dead guard's walkie-talkie and tried to call someone. After a few minutes, Ellie answered.

'Thank God, you're safe,' she said. 'Are the children all right?'

'Yes, they're with me and they're OK too.'

'Listen, Alan,' Ellie said, 'the raptors are free from their enclosure. They've killed people and they're all around the building. You were lucky to get in. I'm with Wu and Harding in the Control Room. Muldoon is outside and he's just called us on his walkie-talkie. He's trying to get back. He went with Gennaro and Arnold to the generator building. They were trying to turn the main power on again. Arnold never came back. Gennaro went to help Arnold but he hasn't come back either.'

As Grant was speaking to Ellie, the park warden came in through the doors. He had an injured foot.

'Muldoon's here,' said Grant.

'The raptors are on the roof,' said Muldoon. 'We aren't safe here. The raptors will break though the metal bars on the skylights.'

'Can they get through those thick bars?' asked Grant.

'Yes, easily,' replied Muldoon. 'We have to get the power back on so those bars are electrified again.'

'I'll go to the generator building,' said Grant. 'You take the kids to Dr Wu in the Control Room. I've got a walkie-talkie. Wu will have to read the instructions on the printout. He'll have to tell me what to do.'

A few minutes later, Grant was in the generator building. He had his torch with him.

'I'm in,' he said to Wu on the walkie-talkie. 'And I've found Gennaro. He's OK. We're in front of the generator now. What do we do?'

'Find two large buttons, one red and one yellow. Press the yellow button down, then press the red one.'

There was a humming sound and the generator started working again.

'Why haven't the lights come on?' asked Grant.

'The power will be on in the Control Room now that the generator is on,' replied Wu. 'But everything else has to be reset from the computer in the Control Room. Get back there and I'll tell you what to do then.'

'Aren't you in the Control Room?'

'No. I'm down by the main door of the Visitors' Centre now. Harding, Muldoon and Ellie are with me. There are raptors in the section between you the and Visitors' Centre. You can't get back unless we help you. We're going to make a lot of noise. The raptors will follow us to the Safari Lodge. You will be able to get back without them seeing you. Then you can switch the system on and we can get back too.

'Tim and Lex are in the Control Room. They are safer there. Good luck!'

Wu switched off his walkie-talkie. He turned towards the others by the main door of the Visitors' Centre.

'OK,' said Muldoon. 'Dr Sattler, Wu, Harding, make a lot of noise and go towards the Lodge. Get inside before the raptors are together and ready to attack.'

They all reached the door of the Safari Lodge safely – Ellie, Muldoon, Harding and Wu. The raptors followed. But as soon as the people were inside the building, the raptors turned round and started to walk away.

'They know what we're doing – don't they?' asked Ellie.

'They're very intelligent,' said Muldoon. 'No, Ellie don't!' he shouted, as Ellie ran outside again. She was waving her arms and shouting.

The raptors turned again. One and then another jumped towards her and away again. But they didn't attack.

Suddenly, the men in the doorway saw why the raptors were doing this. A third raptor jumped down from the roof and landed behind Ellie. Wu ran out of the door and the raptor turned towards him. Harding ran out and pulled Ellie inside. Ellie was safe, but they couldn't save Wu. They could do nothing as the raptors' sharp claws cut his body.

13

Power On

Tim and Lex were alone in the Control Room. There was nothing for them to do. Then things began to change. Lights appeared on the big glass map. There were humming noises and the computer screens shone bright green.

'Look, Lex. The power must be on again,' said Tim.

At the top of one of the screens was written the time: 10:47:22. Thirteen minutes before the supply ship would arrive in San José! They had to contact the ship soon.

One screen said: JURASSIC PARK – SYSTEM START-UP. Tim

knew a little about computers. Could he make the system work?

There was a noise behind Tim. He turned and saw that Lex was holding a walkie-talkie. Muldoon's voice suddenly spoke. 'What's happening?'

Tim spoke into the walkie-talkie.

'This is Tim, Mr Muldoon. Lex and I are in the Control Room. Can you tell me how to get the computer system working again?'

'I'm sorry, Tim. No one here knows anything about it. I'm in the Safari Lodge with Dr Sattler, Dr Harding and Mr Hammond. Dr Grant and Mr Gennaro should get back to the Control Room soon. Mr Arnold and Dr Wu can't help.

'Please try to do something, Tim. There are raptors in the corridors here. And two of them are biting through the bars over the skylights on the roof. Unless the bars are electrified again soon ... well ... we haven't got long before the raptors get in.'

'OK. I'll try,' said Tim.

He switched off the walkie-talkie and sat down in front of the computer screen. He pressed keys on the keyboard but nothing happened. Then he touched the screen and it changed. Words appeared. Good. Now he knew how to make the computer do things.

He touched the word: VIEW and the video screens showed camera pictures from all over the park. One screen showed the raptors who were biting the bars of the skylights in the Lodge. Another screen showed the supply ship. It was very near to the dock at San José. There wasn't much time left!

Tim touched GRID RESET on the computer screen. The screen changed to show a map of the park and buildings. He touched SAFARI LODGE. Perhaps he could get the power into the fences and metal bars again and kill the raptors on the roof. But the screen gave a message: COMMAND IMPOSSIBLE. What was he going to do now?

'Tim! Come quickly!' screamed Lex, who was standing by the door.

'No, not now, Lex. Be quiet!' he shouted at her.

'Tim – come here now!' Lex screamed.

He ran to the door and heard hissing noises which were not far away. Slowly, he opened the door and went out. Lex followed him. There, at one end of the corridor, were three raptors. The children turned to go back into the Control Room. But the door was shut and locked! The security locks were working again!

Tim saw a security guard lying at the other end of the corridor. 'Come on,' he whispered.

The children ran along the corridor and took the guard's security card which was on his belt. But the raptors had seen them. The three animals were getting ready to attack.

'In here,' said Tim, and he opened the nearest door with the security card and pushed Lex into the room. Then he pushed her through another door, then another and back out into the corridor. They could hear the noise of the raptors following them. Lex and Tim ran as fast as they could – straight into something! Lex screamed in terror.

'It's OK, kids,' said a voice.

Grant and Gennaro were standing in front of them. The raptors stopped when they saw more people.

Grant pushed the children towards Gennaro. 'Take them to the Control Room,' he said.

'What are you going to do?' asked Gennaro.

'I've got a plan. Now, go.'

———

When they were back in the Control Room, Tim sat down in front of the computer screen again.

'I can't make the power come on,' he said to Gennaro.

'I know what to do,' answered Gennaro. 'You have to tell the system to use the *main* electrical power again. It starts up on emergency power.'

Tim read everything on the screen. Then he touched ELECTRICAL MAIN. A message said: MAIN POWER ACTIVATED[110]. Then Tim touched GRID RESET again and SAFARI LODGE.

They all looked at the video screen which showed the roof of the Safari Lodge. Sparks and smoke were coming from the bodies of the raptors there. The bars were electrified again!

ACTIVATED, said the message on the screen.

'You did it! You did it!' shouted Gennaro.

'The ship!' said Lex. 'What about the ship?'

They looked back at the other screen and saw that the ship was going into the dock at San José. Tim touched the screen again and again. He found details about the ship. He found the phone link to the ship and pressed the screen.

'Hello, Captain here,' said a voice. 'Is that Mr Arnold?'

Gennaro spoke. 'Captain, this is Donald Gennaro. You must *not* stop at San José. You must return to Isla Nublar. You have some dangerous animals on your ship.'

'I don't know who you are,' said the captain. 'But I take orders from Mr Arnold.'

'Turn the ship round immediately,' said Gennaro loudly. 'If you don't you will be arrested. Don't you know section 509 of the Uniform Oceans Act?'

'OK, I understand,' said the captain.

On the screen, they saw the ship move backwards away from the dock.

'What's the Uniform Oceans Act?' asked Grant, as he came into the Control Room.

'I don't know,' said Gennaro. 'But I made the captain turn his ship around!'

Gennaro then used the phone to make some more calls. He called his boss in San Francisco and he called the authorities in San José. Now, Isla Nublar had to be destroyed. Soldiers and helicopters would come to the island to kill the dinosaurs.

'Where are the three raptors now, Dr Grant?' asked Tim.

'They're dead, Tim. Do you remember the syringes full of poison we saw yesterday in the Fertilization Room? Dr Wu showed them to us.'

'Yes.'

'Well – I made the raptors follow me into the Fertilization Room. I injected poison from the syringes into some eggs. Then I rolled the eggs towards the raptors when they came in the door.

'The raptors came into the room slowly. Two raptors ate the eggs and died immediately. The third raptor attacked me, but I managed to inject it with a syringe of poison. So they're all dead.'

'The raptors on the roof are dead, too,' said Tim.

'Good,' said Grant. 'I don't think there are any others near here.'

The door opened and Muldoon, Ellie and Harding came in. In less than 24 hours many people had died in Jurassic Park – security guards and workmen, Nedry, Regis, Malcolm,

'I injected poison into some eggs. Then I rolled the eggs towards the raptors.'

Wu and Arnold.

'We must find out where the other raptors are,' said Ellie.
'Can you find out from the computer, Tim?'

Tim was good at using the computer now. Soon the screen
showed the numbers of animals in the park.

Total Animals	292	
Species	Expected	Found
Tyrannosaurs	2	1
Maiasaurs	22	20
Stegosaurs	4	1
Triceratops	8	6
Compsognathids	65	64
Othnielia	23	15
Velociraptors	37	27
Apatosaurs	17	12
Hadrosaurs	11	5
Dilophosaurs	7	4
Pterosaurs	6	5
Hypsilophodontids	34	14
Euoplocephalids	16	9
Styracosaurs	18	7
Callovosaurs	22	13
Total	292	203

'What's happening now?' asked Gennaro. 'Why are
there fewer animals?'

'Jurassic Park is coming under control,' said Ellie.

'I don't understand,' said Gennaro.

'The electric fences weren't working for many hours. Look
what's happening,' said Grant, pointing at the video screens.
'The park is becoming a real Jurassic world. The animals are
behaving as they did millions of years ago. The meat-eaters
are killing the plant-eaters. I think the last raptors from the
enclosure are in the park with the raptors who were born

there.'

One video screen showed a group of raptors chasing some hypsilophodontids. On another screen, six raptors had jumped on a huge hadrosaur. They were biting it and cutting it with their sharp claws. The young tyrannosaur was hunting a stegosaur. The triceratops were fighting each other.

Everyone in the Control Room watched silently.

14

Control of the Island

The raptor hunters

Four hours had passed. It was late afternoon. The computer was working properly. The Visitors' Centre and the Safari Lodge were safe. Soldiers were coming from Costa Rica in helicopters. Three young raptors had been found on the supply ship and they had been killed. Grant and Ellie, Gennaro, Muldoon, Harding and the children were waiting in the Control Room.

'Grant, when the soldiers come, they'll bomb the island and burn everything on the ground,' said Muldoon suddenly. 'Do you want to go into the park and find the raptors' nests before it gets dark?'

'Yes, I do,' replied Grant. 'What kind of weapons have we got?'

'We've got some long electric prods. They will hurt anything you touch with them.

'And I've found some gas bombs which paralyze animals.

Hammond had hidden them in the storeroom. He didn't want us to find them and use them.'

Ellie was looking at the glass map on the wall.

'The raptors must be in the south of the island,' she said. 'There's a big underground pool of water there. I think the raptors like water and darkness. I think they'll be there.'

'I think you're right,' said Grant. 'Now, kids, I want you to stay here with Dr Harding while we go to find the nests.'

Muldoon, Grant, Gennaro and Ellie went to the garage under the Visitors' Centre. The little raptor that Grant had found in the tunnel was in a cage. It was frightened of them and its colour changed to green and then back to brown again.

'It must be a wild animal that was born in the park,' said Muldoon. 'The ones we made in the laboratory didn't change colour.' Then he remembered something. 'Grant, how did they breed in the park? We only made female dinosaurs. There were no males.'

'Wu used parts of frog DNA to repair the dinosaur DNA,' replied Grant. 'And some frogs can change from female to male. If there is a group of frogs that is all female, some of them will become male so they can breed.'

'And that's what happened to the dinosaurs?'

'Yes, I think so. Let's go and find the raptors' nests.'

Grant lifted the raptor out of its cage.

'Go away! Go home!' he said.

The little raptor ran away towards the forest. They all got into the Jeep. And Ellie drove after the raptor.

Soon they could hear the sound of the ocean. The little raptor ran along paths and among the trees. Then suddenly it climbed up onto a rock and disappeared.

The little raptor ran along paths and among the trees.

Ellie stopped the Jeep and they all got out. Among the rocks there was a hole. Squeaking sounds came from the hole – the noises of many animals.

Ellie went to the Jeep and brought back a torch and some night-vision goggles. Grant got down onto the ground and pushed himself backwards into the hole. Ellie gave the torch and goggles to Grant.

'Follow me,' he said to her. Then suddenly he disappeared into the hole.

———

Hammond

Hammond had been in the Safari Lodge for some time. It was quiet outside now. He was sure it was safe to go out. He walked along a path and out into the park. It was the end of the afternoon and the sun was getting lower in the sky.

Everything would be all right now. Gennaro had called the army to bomb the park from helicopters. The army was going to burn everything. But Hammond's work was safe. He had more dinosaur embryos. They were in a secret place in the USA. He could buy another island. He could start a new park somewhere else in the world.

When the tyrannosaur roared, Hammond turned round so quickly that he fell down onto the path. He thought that he saw the young rex in the thick bushes beside the path. Why was the tyrannosaur here? Why was it outside its enclosure?

Hammond jumped up and ran. He ran up a steep hill and into the forest. It was darker in the forest and there was soft, wet mud under his feet. He fell again and rolled over and over down the hill. At last he stopped moving. He tried to stand up but there was a terrible pain in his foot. His foot was broken.

The children

Tim and Lex were alone in the Control Room.

'I wanted to go and find the dinosaurs' nests,' said Lex.

'It's too dangerous. We've got to stay here,' said Tim. 'Hey, listen to this, Lex.'

Tim pressed a button and the sound of a tyrannosaur's roar came out of the loudspeakers in the park.

'That was great!' said Lex excitedly. 'That was a better roar than the first one, Tim. Can I do it now?'

'Yes,' said Tim. 'Push this button here ... Then we'll try the other button.'

Hammond

Hammond heard the tyrannosaur roar again as he lay at the bottom of the hill. He was frightened. What would the rex do? He couldn't climb the hill again because of his broken foot. He decided to wait until the animal had gone. Then he would shout for help.

Then Hammond heard Lex's voice over the loudspeaker. 'Let me press the button again, Tim. I want to make the noise.'

Lex and Tim! His grandchildren were playing in the Control Room. The real tyrannosaur hadn't roared. Hammond was angry, but he was afraid too. He sat and listened to the sounds of the forest. Then he started to shout for help.

No one came.

At last, Hammond decided to try and climb back up the hill to find a path. After an hour, he still had not reached the top. He had to move on his left leg because his right foot was so painful. He was hot and thirsty and he was tired.

Hammond heard a squeaking sound which got louder and louder. A small green animal came down the hill towards him – then another – then another. Compys!

Compys were poisonous. They bit animals which were hurt and killed them with poison. Hammond was suddenly terrified. He picked up a rock and threw it.

'Get away!' he shouted.

The compys squeaked but they didn't run away. They knew he couldn't hurt them.

Hammond started to climb the hill again. But one of the compys jumped onto his back. He tried to get the animal off. But he fell and rolled down the hill again. A compy jumped onto his hand and bit it. Then another compy jumped onto his back and bit his neck. All the compys started to move closer to him.

The poison started to work and Hammond began to fall asleep. When the next compy jumped on him, he couldn't push it away. When another compy started to bite his neck, he didn't feel much pain.

15

The End of the Park

After Grant had disappeared into the velociraptors' hole, Ellie pushed herself backwards into the hole too.

'Here, take this,' said Muldoon to Gennaro. He gave him one of the electric prods. 'I can't climb down there. I'll have to wait up here.'

Gennaro was very frightened but he climbed down into the darkness. He fell onto a concrete floor.

'Are you OK?' Ellie whispered.

'Yes. Why are you whispering?'

'Look,' she said.

Gennaro stood up and looked around him. Everywhere there were eyes. Green eyes shining in the darkness.

They were in an enormous underground room. A tunnel went away from one side of the room. Gennaro, Ellie and Grant were standing on a concrete ledge about 60 cm above the ground. Below them were about 30 velociraptors. Gennaro kept very quiet.

Grant had put on the night-vision goggles.

'I've been counting,' he said. 'There are 33 raptors here. 6 are adults. I think there are 5 babies here and 22 young ones – the babies born last year. And there are 3 nests.'

'There's something strange about the young raptors,' said Ellie. 'Watch them. They play and turn around then suddenly they stop. They all stand and look at the wall. The adults stand and look at the wall too.'

Grant watched. Ellie was right.

'Why are they doing that?' Gennaro asked.

Suddenly the young raptors began to squeak and run around excitedly. The adult raptors watched. And then, making lots of noise, all the dinosaurs ran in the same direction. They ran down the concrete tunnel into the darkness.

Ellie, Gennaro and Grant ran down the concrete tunnel after the dinosaurs. Suddenly, they were out on the shore of the Pacific Ocean. Behind them, they could hear the humming noise of the electric fence.

'Well, now we know how they get out of the enclosure,' said Ellie. 'But why did they do that? Why did they run down to the ocean?'

Then Ellie, Grant and Gennaro heard the sound of a ship's engine. A ship slowly appeared out of the fog and went past the island.

'Did the raptors come out because they heard the ship's engine?' asked Gennaro.

'I guess so,' said Grant.

But why have they done it? Grant thought.

He looked at the raptors. They were standing on the shore looking at the ocean.

These animals are so like birds, he thought.

Birds! Suddenly Grant understood what he was looking at.

'They want to leave,' he said. 'They are behaving like birds. They want to migrate[111].'

'Migrate!' repeated Ellie. 'Of course. That's fantastic! No one has ever known that about dinosaurs.'

'No, they haven't,' said Grant, smiling.

Then suddenly, several huge helicopters came out of the fog towards them. Their engines made a loud noise. The velociraptors ran away and disappeared.

One of the helicopters landed on the beach and soldiers jumped out and ran towards the three people.

A soldier shouted, 'Please come with us now! Quickly!'

The soldiers pulled Gennaro, Grant and Ellie into the helicopter. They pushed them into seats and the helicopter took off. Muldoon, Harding and the children were sitting inside. Lex and Tim looked very small and very tired. Lex was lying against her brother.

The raptors were standing on the shore looking at the ocean.

Muldoon shouted to Grant, Ellie and Gennaro, 'The soldiers want us out of here. They're going to bomb the island now!'

The helicopter flew up and away from the beach. Grant looked down out of the open door but he could not see any of the raptors. Then he shouted to Muldoon.

'What happened to Hammond?'

Muldoon shouted back, 'Hammond is dead. We found him on a hill near the Safari Lodge. The compys killed him.'

Grant was too tired to feel sorry for Hammond. He turned away and looked out of the helicopter door again. It was getting dark now. He saw the young tyrannosaur by the shore of the lake. It was eating a hadrosaur and it had blood on its jaws.

Suddenly there were explosions. Below them, bombs were exploding. The Visitors' Centre was burning. Bright orange flames covered the building. Grant saw hypsilophodontids running through the forest. Then there was another explosion and he couldn't see them any more.

Grant thought of the raptors standing on the beach. Where had they wanted to migrate to? He would never know.

A soldier spoke to him.

'Are you in charge of Isla Nublar?'

'No,' Grant replied.

'Please, sir, who is in charge?'

'Nobody,' said Grant.

The helicopter flew across the ocean towards Costa Rica. Grant looked back once more at Isla Nublar. Fog covered the island and it was almost night now. But through the fog and the darkness, Grant saw bright white explosions. It looked as if the whole of Jurassic Park was on fire.

Points for Understanding

1

1 What do Dr Alan Grant and Dr Ellie Sattler do?
2 What do you learn about John Hammond in this chapter?
3 Who is Donald Gennaro? What information did Grant give to Donald Gennaro?
4 Grant is sent a fax of an X-ray. Why is he surprised by it?
5 Why does Hammond phone Grant?

2

1 Donald Gennaro talks to his boss.
   (a)   Why is Gennaro worried?
   (b)   Who is going to Isla Nublar?
2 Ellie and Grant look at the map of Isla Nublar. Why does Ellie say it is like a zoo?
3 Who flies to Isla Nublar with Hammond?
4 Why does the man from InGen Incorporated meet the lawyer from the Biosyn Corporation?
5 Professor Malcolm says things will start to go wrong and continue to go wrong.
   (a)   What is the theory that he studies?
   (b)   Which place is he talking about?

3

1 Why is Dennis Nedry going to Isla Nublar?
2 'It's beautiful. It moves so gracefully.'
   What is Ellie talking about?
3 'This is like a prison and I want to know why.'
   What is Grant talking about?
4 'You are experts and I want your opinions.'
   What does Gennaro want to know?
5 Who arrives in the helicopter?
6 Why is Gennaro angry?

4

1 Who is in the Control Room? What are their jobs?
2 What does Dr Wu remove from pieces of amber?
3 What do the Cray XMP supercomputers do?
4 What happens in the Fertilization Room?
5 How many live dinosaurs are there in the park? How many different species are there?
6 Who is Tim's 'new friend'?
7 Why has the ship come to the dock in the north of the island?
8 Ellie and Grant, Malcolm and Tim were shocked. Why?

5

1 What is shown on the huge glass map?
2 Why are there sensors and video cameras in the park?
3 How many generators are there?
4 Why is Hammond angry with
  (a)   Muldoon?
  (b)   Wu?
  (c)   Nedry?

6

1 What does Tim find when he looks around inside his land-cruiser?
2 Which dinosaurs do Tim and Lex see on the tour? Describe two of them.
3 What does Tim see running among the sauropods?
4 Grant finds something when they stop to look at the stegosaur. What does he find?
5 The computer program counted the number of animals in the park. But it got the wrong number. What was wrong with the program?
6 Why is Grant so worried?

7

1 Who travels in the first land-cruiser? Who travels in the second land-cruiser?
2 Why has Nedry decided to steal the embryos?
3 What goes wrong with Nedry's plan?
4 What does the dilophosaur do to Nedry?

8

1 What does Lex see on the supply ship?
2 'Oh God,' said Regis. His body started to shake. He was terrified.
  (a) Why was he terrified?
  (b) What did he do?
3 The tyrannosaur picked up the land-cruiser.
  What happened to Lex? What happened to Tim?
4 What did the rex do to Malcolm?
5 What killed Ed Regis?
6 Where did Grant and the children sleep that night?

9

1 Why does Muldoon want to go out in the Jeep?
2 The men suddenly understood what had happened.
  What have they understood?
3 'We've been out on the tour road in the Jeep,' says Muldoon to Arnold.
  What information does Muldoon give Arnold?
4 Why does Arnold shut down the computer system and restart it?

10

1 Why do the hadrosaurs start to run and cry out in fear?
2 What do Grant and the children take from the shed?
3 What happens when Lex coughs?
4 Grant and the children see two dilophosaurs. What is strange about them?

11

1 What does Muldoon do to the big tyrannosaur?
2 The three of them fell too – down and down and down.
  What has happened?
3 How do Grant and the children try to escape from the big
  tyrannosaur?
4 What does Grant find behind the metal door?
5 What happens to Tim?
6 Why does the big rex fall down?
7 What goes wrong with the power supply? What problems does
  this cause?

12

1 What happens to Arnold in the generator building?
2 Who goes into the generator building next?
3 'We're going to make a lot of noise. The raptors will follow us to
  the Safari Lodge.'
  (a)   Who is speaking?
  (b)   What is his plan?
  (c)   What goes wrong?

13

1 Tim tries to reset the computer system. Why must he hurry? Give
  two reasons.
2 How do Tim and Lex escape from the raptors in the corridor?
3 Why does the captain turn the supply ship round?
4 How does Grant kill the three raptors?
5 'Why are there fewer animals?' asks Gennaro.
  What is he talking about? How does Grant answer him?

14

1 What do Muldoon, Gennaro, Ellie and Grant decide to do?
2 'Grant, how did they breed in the park?' asks Muldoon.
  What was Grant's reply?
3 What happens to Hammond?

15

1 Ellie, Grant and Gennaro go into an underground room and find
  the raptors' nests. What is strange about the animals' behaviour?
2 Where do the raptors go?
3 What does Grant suddenly understand about the raptors?
4 When he is in the helicopter, what does Grant learn from
  Muldoon?

Tyrannosaurus rex
/tɪˌrænəˌsɔːrəs ˈreks/

Stegosaur
/ˈstegəsɔː/

Maiasaur
/maɪəsɔː/

Compsognathus
/kɒmpsɒgˈneɪθəs/

Othnielia
/ɒθnɪˈelɪə/

Triceratops
/traɪˈserətɒps/

Velociraptor
/vəlɒsɪˈræptə/

116

Pterosaur
/'terəsɔː/

Hadrosaur
/'hædrəsɔː/

Apatosaur
/ə'pætəsɔː/

Hypsilophodon
/hɪpsɪlɒfə'dɒn/

Euoplocephalus
/juːɒplə'kefələs/

Dilophosaur
/dɪ'lɒfəsɔː/

Styracosaur
/staɪ'rækəsɔː/

Microceratops
/maɪkrəʊ'serətɒps/

117

Glossary

1 **paleontologists** (page 4)
[/pælɪɒn'tɒlɒdʒɪsts/] paleo = old. ontologist = someone who studies life. Paleontologists are scientists who study the history of life on Earth.

2 **fossils** (page 4)
plants or animals that have been dug from the ground. The plants or animals lived millions of years ago and have now become hard like stone.

3 **paleobotanists** (page 4)
[/ˌpælɪəʊ'bɒtəənɪsts/] botany = the study of plants. Paleobotanists are scientists who study how plants lived and grew many millions of years ago.

4 **behave** – to behave (page 5)
do things in a certain way. People want to know how dinosaurs lived in early times. Was their behaviour gentle and quiet? Or were they fierce and violent?

5 **lawyer** (page 6)
someone who studies the law and gives people advice about the law.

6 **Environmental Protection Agency** (page 6)
an organization in this story that makes sure that companies and industries do not make or do things that could harm the world.

7 **computer expert** (page 6)
an expert is someone who knows a lot about something. A computer expert knows all about computers – how they work and how they can be used.

8 **mathematician** (page 7)
someone who studies problems and numbers. A mathematician uses this knowledge to find out how things work.

9 **publicity manager** (page 7)
a person whose job is to tell people all about a company and its work.

10 **chief engineer** (page 7)
a person whose job is to look after all the machinery and technical equipment in a company.

11 **park warden** (page 8)
a person who makes sure that the animals in an animal park are safe, well and have enough to eat. The warden also looks after the other workers in the park.

12 **chief geneticist** (page 8)
every living thing has cells in its body. In each tiny cell there are *genes*. Genes control how the living thing will grow and how it will be different from a similar plant, animal or creature. *Genetics* is the study and identification of genes in the cells of different living things. A *geneticist* is a scientist who studies genes from cells. *Genetical engineering* is when genes are taken from a cell, copied and altered to make new cells.

13 **vet** (veterinary surgeon) (page 8)
an animal doctor.

14 **waving** – *to wave* (page 9)
hold up your hand and move it up and down. You wave to say hello or good-bye to someone. You also wave to make someone look towards you.

15 **amber** (page 11)
a hard yellow stone that is made from the *sap* of trees that lived millions of years ago. Sap is a liquid that carries the food around inside plants and trees.

16 **connection with** (page 11)
when two things work together or are used together.

17 **Cray XMP supercomputers** (page 12)
some of the most powerful and expensive computers in the world.

18 **Hood gene sequencers** (page 12)
computers that look at the genes taken from cells. (See Glossary No. 12)

19 **samples of DNA** (page 12)
these letters are the initials for DeoxyriboNucleic Acid [/dɪˌɒksɪraɪbəʊnjuːˌkleɪk ˈæsɪd/]. All living things have cells which contain genes. Each gene is made of DNA. In a diagram, DNA looks like a chain. A sample of DNA is a piece of DNA that has been removed so that a scientist can study it.

20 **fax** (page 13)

a letter or picture that is sent by a machine. The machine copies the message exactly. In this way people can send important papers to each other in a few minutes.

21 **x-ray** (page 13)

a photograph which shows the bones inside a creature's body.

22 **Triassic Period** (page 13)

[/traɪˈæsɪk/] between about 245 and 193 million years ago.

23 **compsognathus** (page 13)

[/kɒmpsɒgˈneɪθəs/] plural = *compsognathids*. *Compy* is the short name used in this book. See page 116.

24 **real** (page 13)

Ellie cannot believe that this is the x-ray of a living animal. There are no dinosaurs alive today.

25 **Jurassic Period** (page 13)

[/dʒʊˈræsɪk/] between about 193 and 136 million years ago. A few species of dinosaurs were living in the *Cretaceous Period* [/krəˈteɪʃəs/]. The Cretaceous Period was between about 136 and 64 million years ago. At the end of the Cretaceous Period all the large dinosaurs had died.

26 **crocodiles and sharks** (page 13)

crocodiles are meat-eating reptiles that live in rivers. Crocodiles have thick skin, long tails and sharp teeth. Sharks are meat-eating fish that live in the sea. Sharks have sharp teeth and can swim very quickly.

27 **resort and animal park** (page 14)

a place where people can go and stay and see animals living in very large enclosures.

28 **computer systems** (page 15)

a system is a way of doing something. A computer system is the way a computer works and makes other things work for it. For example, the computer system at Jurassic Park controls all the power and keeps records of all the animals.

29 **invested** – *to invest* (page 15)

use money to buy something so you will make more money. Rich people and big companies have given John Hammond money to build his park. When Hammond receives money from visitors, some of this money will be given to the people and companies who invested money in the park.

30 *sort out the bugs in the computer system* (page 16)
computers have memories which have been made or *programmed*. The *programs* are written by computer scientists. If a program goes wrong, mistakes occur in the way the computer does its work. These mistakes in the program are called bugs. When bugs get into the computer they must be removed – sorted out – quickly. If they are not removed the computer will go wrong and stop working. It will *fail*.

31 *sections* (page 16)
areas of land with fences around them.

32 *concrete moats* (page 16)
water is mixed with sand and limestone to make concrete. Concrete becomes very hard when it is dry. Moats are deep, wide ditches that are dug around buildings. Sometimes moats are filled with water. Moats make it difficult for people or animals to move from one place to another.

33 *electric fences* (page 16)
the tall fences and windows of Jurassic Park are made of metal. Very powerful electricity is sent through the metal. It is *electrified*. If something touches these fences or windows that person or animal will feel pain.

34 *embryos of all 15 species* (page 17)
an embryo is a very young creature that has just started to grow from an egg. Species are types of animal. For example, a lion is a species of cat.

35 *shaving foam* (page 17)
soft, white soap with air in it. Men use shaving foam when they cut (shave) their beards.

36 *dock* (page 18)
the place on a river or by the sea where boats and ships stop. Goods are loaded onto or unloaded from ships at a dock. Passengers can also get on or off ships.

37 *complex system* (page 20)
something which has many different parts. All these parts work in lots of different ways. The system is complex because you cannot easily guess how the parts will work on their own or together. A *simple system* has fewer parts and scientists can understand more easily how each part works and where it belongs. When scientists *do an experiment on a complex system* they look at the parts and try to make changes happen. In this way they can study that system.

38 **predict** – *to predict* (page 20)

try to guess what will happen to something in the future. *Unpredictable changes* are the changes that no one thought would happen. People make *predictions* when they say what they think will happen in the future.

39 **curved** (page 21)

not straight. If something *curves* it bends round.

40 **billions** (page 22)

thousands of millions. UK = a million millions (1 000 000 000 000). US = a thousand millions (1 000 000 000).

41 **trumpeting** – *trumpeting sound* (page 22)

a sound like the noise made by an elephant.

42 **apatosaurs** (page 22)

[/əˈpætəsɔːz/] singular = *apatosaur*. See page 117.

43 **skylights** (page 24)

windows in the roof.

44 **tour** (page 24)

a journey around the park. During the journey, someone will tell them about the park.

45 **two-storeyed building** (page 24)

a building with two floors.

46 **model of a tyrannosaurus rex** (page 25)

[/tɪˌrænəˌsɔːrəs ˈreks/] plural = *tyrannosaurs*. *Tyrannosaur* = singular, is also used in this book. See page 116. A model is a copy of a dinosaur that has been made out of wood, metal or plastic.

47 **security systems** (page 25)

the security systems lock the doors and windows, put electricity into the fences and make sure the animals are in their enclosures. The computer in Jurassic Park has a program which makes the security systems work.

48 **authorized** – *authorized people* (page 27)

people who have permission.

49 **Extractions** (page 27)

a room where substances are extracted, or removed, from things. (See Glossary No. 19)

50 **security card** (page 27)

a special card made of plastic that opens locked doors.

51 **microscopes** (page 27)

instruments used by scientists to make very small things look bigger.

52 **needle** (page 28)
   a very thin metal tube with a hole through the centre. The blood is
   pulled up through the needle and taken from the fly.
53 **humming** – *humming sound* (page 28)
   a sound like a noise made by a bee.
54 **pressed some keys on the computer keyboard** (page 30)
   the numbers or letters you press to work a computer are called
   keys. They are on a keyboard.
55 **Fertilization** (page 30)
   the room where cells from male creatures and female dinosaurs
   are put into the eggs. Then embryos start to grow.
56 **syringes** (page 30)
   instruments which have a long thin needle at one end and a clear
   plastic tube at the other. Doctors use syringes to *inject* liquid into,
   or to take blood out of peoples' bodies.
57 **Hatchery** (page 30)
   the room where the dinosaurs are hatched – come out of eggs and
   are born.
58 **rows** (page 30)
   things put together in a line.
59 **incubators** (page 31)
   special containers used to keep very young or ill babies warm.
60 **stripes** (page 31)
   long coloured marks on the dinosaur's skin. See illustration on
   page 116.
61 **velociraptors** (page 31)
   [/vəlɒsɪˈræptəz/] singular = *velociraptor*. *Raptor* is the short name
   used in this book. See page 116.
62 **squeaked** – *to squeak* (page 31)
   make a sharp high sound like the noise made by a mouse.
63 **breed** – *to breed* (page 31)
   have babies.
64 **droppings** (page 33)
   faeces or manure.
65 **sensors and video cameras** (page 33)
   sensors are instruments that record when something moves past
   them. Each time an animal (or person) moves past a sensor, a message is sent back to the control system in the computer. Video
   cameras record pictures onto film and show them on TV screens.

66 *generator* (page 34)

a machine that makes electricity.

67 *sparks* (page 35)

bright flashes of light that are made by electricity.

68 *sector* (page 38)

a part of the park. The sectors in Jurassic Park are given numbers. All these sectors are checked by the computer using the sensors and video cameras.

69 *tranquillizer guns* (page 39)

guns which use special *tranquillizer darts*. The darts have a needle at one end. The needle goes into the skin of the animal. Then liquid goes into the animal's body. This *tranquillizer* liquid does not kill the animal. But it makes it fall to the ground and sleep. The animal is *tranquillized*.

70 *batches* (page 39)

groups of animals that were made by the scientists at different times.

71 *dilophosaur* (page 41)

[/dɪˈlɒfəsɔː/] plural = *dilophosaurs*. See page 117.

72 *spit* – *to spit* (page 41)

send sticky liquid out of the mouth.

73 *break down* – *to break down* (page 42)

go wrong and stop working properly.

74 *loudspeaker* (page 43)

an instrument which sends out sounds, voices, etc.

75 *land-cruisers* (page 43)

large cars that can travel easily on rough, difficult ground.

76 *Jeeps* (page 43)

vehicles that can go easily over rough, difficult ground.

77 *maintenance trucks* (page 43)

large vehicles which are used to carry people or equipment when things are being repaired. A *maintenance building* is where useful equipment is kept.

78 *walkie-talkie* (page 43)

a radio that you carry with you. You can only speak to another person who also has a similar walkie-talkie.

79 *linked* – *to be linked to* (page 43)

be connected to.

80 *hypsilophodontids* (page 44)
[/hɪpsɪlɒfə'dɒntɪds/] singular = *hypsilophodon*. See page 117.
81 *spots* (page 44)
round coloured marks on the dinosaur's skin. See the illustration on page 117.
82 *crests* (page 44)
tall thin pieces of skin or bone on top of the dinosaur's head. See the illustration on page 117.
83 *triceratops* (page 44)
[/traɪ'serətɒps/] singular = *triceratops*. See page 116.
84 *sauropods* (page 46)
[/'sɔːrəpɒdz/] singular = *sauropod*. The family name for apatosaurs and hadrosaurs.
85 *hadrosaurs* (page 46)
[/'hædrəsɔːz/] singular = *hadrosaur*. See page 117.
86 *spikes* (page 47)
long sharp horns on the dinosaur's body. See the illustration on page 116. These spikes were used when the animals fought.
87 *stegosaur* (page 47)
[/'stegəsɔː/] plural = *stegosaurs*. See page 116.
88 *berries* (page 47)
the fruits on a plant, bush or tree.
89 *maiasaurs* (page 51)
[/'maɪəsɔːz/] singular = *maiasaur*. See page 116.
90 *othnielia* (page 51)
[/ɒθnɪ'elɪə/] singular = *othnielia*. See page 116.
91 *shut down* (page 54)
turn off the power. When the power is turned on again it is *started up*.
92 *crackling* – *crackling noises* (page 58)
noises made by a radio so you cannot hear the words clearly.
93 *wreck* (page 63)
the vehicle has been very badly damaged. It cannot be driven now. It is a wreck.
94 *cough* – *to cough* (page 64)
make a noise when you have something stuck in your throat.
95 *morphine* (page 69)
a powerful drug that is given to people who are in pain.

96 *commands* (page 69)

instructions that are put into a computer program.

97 *reset* (page 70)

working correctly again.

98 *inflatable raft* (page 73)

a boat made of rubber. When the raft is opened up – unfolded – air is blown into it and it is *inflated*. The raft can then carry people on the water.

99 *jetty* (page 74)

a place at the side of a lake or river where boats can be tied up.

100 *snorting and buzzing* (page 74)

buzzing sounds are the noises made by flies or mosquitoes. Snorting sounds are the noises made by a large animal when it blows air through its nose.

101 *rowed* – *to row* (page 75)

move the boat through the water using oars.

102 *microceratops* (page 76)

[/maɪkrəʊˈserətɒps/] plural = *microceratops*. See page 117.

103 *waterfall* (page 82)

the place where a river falls over a tall rock or cliff.

104 *ledge* (page 83)

a narrow shelf of rock or wood.

105 *keypad* (page 83)

groups of numbers on buttons which you press to open a locked door.

106 *printout* (page 86)

when a computer is connected to a printer you can print the information from the screen onto paper. The paper is called a printout.

107 **Wish me luck** (page 89)

Gennaro knows that there is great danger. He is asking the others to give him good fortune.

108 *disaster* (page 91)

a time of terrible bad luck and suffering.

109 *security guard* (page 92)

someone who works in a building where important business is done or where valuable things are kept. Security guards make sure that all doors and windows are safely locked. They also check who comes in and out of the building.

126

110 **activated** (page 97)
    switched on. The main power is now working again.
111 **migrate** – *to migrate* (page 108)

Heinemann English Language Teaching
A division of Heinemann Publishers (Oxford) Ltd
Halley Court, Jordan Hill, Oxford OX2 8EJ

OXFORD MADRID ATHENS PARIS FLORENCE PRAGUE
SÃO PAULO CHICAGO MELBOURNE AUCKLAND
SINGAPORE TOKYO IBADAN GABORONE
JOHANNESBURG PORTSMOUTH (NH)

ISBN 0 435 27348 5

© Michael Crichton 1991
First published in Great Britain in 1991 by the Random Century Group
Arrow paperback edition 1991
Random House, 20 Vauxhall Bridge Road, London SW1V 2SA

This retold version by F. H. Cornish for Heinemann Guided Readers
© Heinemann Publishers (Oxford) Ltd 1995
Design and illustration © Heinemann Publishers (Oxford) Ltd 1995
This edition first published 1995

Illustrated by Donald Harley
Typography by Adrian Hodgkins
Designed by Sue Vaudin
Cover illustration of trademark/logo of Jurassic Park TM and © 1992 Universal
City Studios, Inc. and Amblin Entertainment, Inc. Design by Marketplace Design
Typeset in 11/13.5 pt Goudy
Printed and bound in Malta by Interprint Limited

95 96 97 98 99 10 9 8 7 6 5 4 3 2 1